男孩與海龜的冒險日記

Michael Angelou 著

My Best Friend Looks Like an Island

My Best Friend Looks like an Island
男孩與海龜的冒險日記

Published by Bookman Books, Ltd.
3F, 60, Roosevelt Rd. Sec. 4, Taipei 100, Taiwan

作　　　　者	Michael Angelou
執 行 編 輯	劉怡君
校　　　　對	Lynn Sauvé　Rebecca Lee
插　　　　畫	Tom Liao
出　版　者	書林出版有限公司
	100 台北市羅斯福路四段 60 號 3 樓
	電 話 (02) 2368-4938・2365-8617
	傳真 (02) 2368-8929・2363-6630
台北書林書店	106 台北市新生南路三段 88 號 2 樓之 5
	Tel (02) 2365-8617
學 校 業 務 部	Tel (02) 2368-7226・(04) 2376-3799・(07) 229-0300
經 銷 業 務 部	Tel (02) 2368-4938
發　行　人	蘇正隆
郵　　　　撥	15743873・書林出版有限公司
網　　　　址	http://www.bookman.com.tw
登　記　證	局版臺業字第一八三一號
出 版 日 期	2017 年 2 月
定　　　　價	360 元
I　S　B　N	978-957-445-717-5

For my wife for loving me
and for letting me find my answers in the sea.

Everyone loves stories. Stories make you forget about your own story. We all need time away from our own stories now and then.

Stories can also help you learn a new language. The better the story, the more you'll want to remember. Remember the story and you'll remember the language.

With this book, I hope to give Taiwanese language learners a story that they'll want to remember.

This is not a foreign story. It all happens right here. It happens in Taiwanese places and to Taiwanese people. Since it was made in Taiwan, it is a story that I hope learners can fully relate to. This will bring the characters to life and make the language memorable.

With a bit of luck, learners will even see a bit of themselves and their everyday lives in the story's characters and events. This will keep the characters and events—and the language—alive.

This is a story for Taiwan. This is a story for all the Taiwanese people that have been so good to me over the years.

Thank you.

Chapter

01	Sunday	We all have to come from somewhere...	009
02	Monday	The Seal	017
03	Tuesday	Milkshake	025
04	Wednesday Thursday Friday Saturday	Control	034
05	Sunday Monday	The Heart Sings (Too Loudly)	040
06	Tuesday	Bananas, Books and Bones	054
07	Wednesday Thursday	Dragons	063
08	Friday Saturday Sunday	Fear	071
09	Monday Morning	Another Favor	081
10	Monday afternoon	Escape	087
11	Tuesday	Milkshake Takes the Bait	094
12	Tuesday Evening	Stories	105
13	Wednesday Morning	Tongues, Luck & Yellow Umbrellas	107
14	Wednesday Afternoon	Plans and Apologies	122
15	Still Wednesday Afternoon	What Comes First?	132

Chapter

| 16 | Thursday | Teeth & Freedom | 141 |

| 17 | Friday
Saturday
Saturday Morning | Colors | 151 |

| 18 | Saturday Afternoon | Foreign Chocolate, Ears and English | 155 |

| 19 | Saturday Evening | A Risky Mission Starts | 171 |

| 20 | Saturday Evening | Seconds Later. A Risky Mission Continued... | 179 |

| 21 | Sunday Morning | Guilty Stomachs and Successful Invitations | 193 |

| 22 | Sunday Afternoon | Bubbles | 210 |

| 23 | Later that Sunday Afternoon | Sorry | 212 |

| 24 | Monday | The Sea Welcomes an Old Friend | 219 |

| 25 | Monday Night | Hands | 224 |

| 26 | Tuesday
Tuesday Week
The Tuesday after that | Milkshake Takes the Bait | 227 |

| 27 | Two more Tuesdays after that | Blossoming | 229 |

| 28 | The Tuesday after that | Hats | 238 |

| 29 | Wednesday
Thursday
Friday | Outnumbered | 248 |

| 30 | A Saturday Too | The End. Maybey? | 259 |

Summary:

Kobi is a teenage Taiwanese boy of almost sixteen. He was abandoned by his parents and lives with his grandfather Ye-Ye near the beach in Yilan County. Kobi's best friend is Ro-Ro Gway-Gway (Ro for short) the turtle. Ro taught him how to surf. This is the story of their adventures together, Kobi's first love and the life lessons he learns along the way.

Turtle

Chapter *01* / 🌥 *Sunday*

We all have to come from somewhere...

I really don't mind if it rains. Of course, I like it better when
the sun is shining, but if it's rainy that's okay. Now, if it's
windy, that's a different story. I'm not crazy about the wind.
The wind will play around in your ears and throw dust in your
eyes. Sometimes the wind will also make the sea angry. Then
the water starts to dance around like a mad man, as if all the
molecules are revolting, twisting and turning, and spitting
things out onto the shore. The wind's not always good for
surfing either.

That's me and over there is my turtle, Ro. 'Ro' is short for
'Ro-Ro Gway-Gway'.[1] My grandfather (he should be here in
a minute) called him that because he's a leatherback turtle[2]
and because he loves cinnamon[3] almost as much as he loves
jellyfish.[4] They're called leatherbacks because they don't
really have a hard shell like other turtles. Instead, their backs
feel soft, more like leather or rubber. Ro-Ro Gway-Gway.
My grandfather has always been very clever with words like
that. In fact, he's quite a celebrity in the village for coining
hundreds of new terms that everyone loves and no one can
use properly. He's driven lots of other old people crazy
with these terms. Old people usually don't like new words.
It makes them feel older. One elderly amah[5] heard so many
of Ye-Ye's[6] new words one day that she couldn't handle it.
She went completely mad. Then she went to the temple

We all have to come from somewhere...

What's important is,
Ro made a wrong turn...

and stole someone's fruit offering which was actually meant for Guangong, the god with the red face.[7] She ended up in a lunatic asylum. Afterwards, the whole village scorned her. Not for ending up in a lunatic asylum or for stealing Guangong's pears, but for not eating them and letting them go to waste. Don't worry, everyone said, she'll have to finish them in hell one day along with all the other leftover food she's wasted. Yummy.

Anyway, if he could, Ro would call me Kobi[8] because that's what everyone else calls me. I gave myself that name. Sometimes you just can't trust other people with something so important. My grandfather tried to call me Haidi because I like the sea and sweet potatoes,[9] but I wasn't having any of that. Can you imagine a fifteen- going on sixteen-year-old boy walking around calling himself a name that sounds

like Heidi?! The kids at school would all die laughing. I'd
be at the temple every day going madder and madder and
Guangong would starve to death.

Ro and I are best friends. I confuse him sometimes with my
teenage theories, and he annoys me sometimes because he's
so slow when he's not underwater.[10] But, in general, we get
on like a house on fire.[11] Speaking of which, we currently live
in a small wooden cabin near the beach in Yilan County.[12]
That's on the east coast of the island of Taiwan. Actually
I was born at my grandfather's cottage in Yilan City,[13] but
that burned down when I was five. I don't know where Ro
was born but that's not important. What's important is that
when I was seven, Ro made a wrong turn on his way from
Indonesia[14] to Okinawa[15] and ended up on the beach outside
our new cabin. We led him back out to sea a few times and
showed him the right way to Indonesia, but he kept coming
back for some reason. I guess he just liked us and he's been
with us ever since. He even taught me how to surf. Actually,
he's an amazing surfer. He can...

Wait a minute, we don't even know each other and already
I'm giving away all of Ro's best secrets. That's a trap a lot
of storytellers fall into, even the good ones. Not me. I'm

We all have to come from somewhere...

going to save that for at least the next chapter. First I'll tell
you about our little house. There's not much to report but
there's a while to go yet before we reach the next chapter,
so... Well, first of all, Ro and I share it with my grandfather,
Ye-Ye. We built it together after the family home burned
down about ten years ago. I was only a little boy then but I
know who started the fire. I've just never told anyone.

Ye-Ye is a good man, kind and diligent. He's a good man
because he never cared much about himself. He cares more
about me and about his vegetable garden. Especially his
sweet potato leaves, to Ye-Ye those are like gold flakes.
"Sweet potatoes are for hungry people," he likes to
say, "sweet potato leaves[16] are for happy people. Like
gardeners."
I know he just says that so I don't feel guilty about eating all
the sweet potatoes.

Anyway, it's just as well that Ye-Ye cares so much for me
because, apart from him, there really isn't anybody else
around. My parents went to work in North America when
I was five, leaving me with my grandparents. Now, I've
never been to North America before, but it must be really
picturesque or awesome or something, because it made

them quite forgetful. They forgot all about me! Not even a postcard. Nai-Nai[17]—that's my grandma—didn't forget me but she did get in a boat one day and forgot how to get back. Ye-Ye said the sea only takes the people it loves. I can believe this because Nai-Nai really was a very lovable[18] and affectionate person. I miss her. Ye-Ye does too. Some nights I hear him saying her name in his dreams. Boohoo. Now don't worry, please, all that's in the past. I don't worry about the past because, well, it's not like you can go back and change anything, now can you? The truth

I was a very happy child...
so there's no point in misleading anyone.

We all have to come from somewhere...

is I'm not sad about my parents and Nai-Nai anymore. And I don't want you to start crying in the first chapter or something either! That would be rude. Actually, I was a very happy child and I'm a very happy teenager now, so there's no point in misleading anyone. I've always had Ye-Ye, Ro and the sea and I've always loved all three. They're all easy to love. I think it's because they somehow stay the same even though they're constantly changing. Also, I know they would never leave me because they all have an excellent memory.

I love Sunday mornings too, they're my favorite. They're always slow and peaceful no matter where you are or what you're doing. Sure, sometimes I have to help Ye-Ye around the vegetable patch or the garden, and sometimes I need to make breakfast for the three of us, but mostly Ro and I have the whole morning to ourselves. No school and definitely no time-consuming, tedious homework. Why can't every morning be like Sunday morning?

註 解

1   鞣肉龜桂 is a combination of four Chinese characters: sued
    鞣 , turtle 龜 and cinnamon 肉桂

2   棱皮龜 literally 'wood-beam skin turtle' (詞彙
    leatherback=leather +back)

3   肉桂 literally 'meat laurel'

4   水母 literally 'water mother' (詞彙 jellyfish=jelly+fish)

5   阿嬤 old woman, nurse or grandmother

6   爺爺 paternal grandfather

7   關公 Lord Guan, God of War, Protection & Wealth

8   口筆 literally 'mouth pen'

9   海地 Heidi is pronounced similarly to a combination of
    'sea' and the first word for sweet potato (地瓜 literally 'earth
    melon') 海洋的海＋地瓜的地＝海地 （發音跟著名瑞士小說女主角
    Heidi 一樣）

10 水中的；水面下 underwater (underwater = under+water)

11 片語：(指人) 很快就熟識或關係融洽 'to get on like a house on
    fire'

12 宜蘭縣 a county located on the northeast coast of the
    island of Taiwan

13 宜蘭市 Yilan City, the capital of Yilan County

14 印尼 Indonesia

15 日本沖繩 Japanese islands of Okinawa

16 地瓜葉 sweet potato leaves

17 奶奶 paternal grandmother

18 可愛的，討人喜歡的 (詞彙 loveable = love + able)

Flower

花

Chapter 02 / Monday

The Seal

One of Taiwan's greatest exports is bicycles. We have a geography test later today. I looked up from my textbook.

"Where are you going with that flower, Ro?"

A drowsy Ro was crawling past my door. He was ignoring me for some reason this morning. He does that sometimes when he wakes up on the wrong side of bed.[1] This happens quite frequently, by the way. Often, he'll only really start feeling better once he's caught his first wave of the morning, so I try not to bother him before that. Today, however, I simply couldn't help myself. What was up with the flower?

"Ro's got a girlfriend, Ro's got a girlfriend!" I sang as I danced around him and made silly faces.

Ye-Ye also started chuckling. But Ro just kept crawling along slowly with the tremendous persistence that all turtles are blessed with. He wasn't paying any attention to the two of us. The fact that his progress was so slow his flippers[2] seemed to be made of chewing gum, didn't appear to bug him either. Ye-Ye and I were still giggling by the time Ro had reached the front doorstep. The door was divided into two parts, a top and a bottom half that could open separately. We normally kept the bottom section open

so that Ro would be able to get in and out of the house
easily. He still held the flower stalk firmly in his mouth. As
I watched, I couldn't help thinking that he really was the
most interesting turtle in the world. And his latest interest
in botany made him even more fascinating.
"Hang on, Ro, don't be angry!" I called after him. "I'm
coming, I'm coming!"

Ro's interesting but he really is a bit slow on land, so Ye-Ye
and I built a shortcut[3] for him to the beach. The shortcut is
composed of five long, thick tree trunks. We had to go up
into the mountains and chop down three of them, but the
other two washed up on the beach. We placed the trunks
next to one another in a long line and put stones around
them to keep them steady. Then we shoveled sand into
the gaps between the stones for some additional support.
Finally, we hollowed out the tree trunks to fashion a giant
slide. It's a bit like the ones you see on playgrounds and theme
parks, except much much much cooler. It looks like a giant
canoe! Just a couple of meters outside the front door, Ro can
climb onto an old antique skateboard[4] of mine and ride down
the hollow tree-trunk shortcut to the beach. It looks like so
much fun that I've even tried it once or twice myself.

Unfortunately, the way back up to the house from the beach isn't that high-tech. After a surf, I simply drag Ro behind me on the back of an old broken surfboard[5] with the leash[6] still attached. Turtle transportation isn't rocket science, you know, a primitive sled can do wonders. Plus, Ro seems to enjoy being towed around like a king in his royal chariot. We call the chariot the 'Ro-Mobile'. Ye-Ye's really very proud of designing the slide and thinking of the sled. Both of them have saved Ro so much time. And time, as Ye-Ye reminds me (time after time), is the one thing you can never get back.

By the time I had ducked under the top part of the door, Ro had already slid off the old skateboard and onto the wet sandy beach. I ran down past the vegetable garden and the tree trunks.
"Hey, you have to get ready for school, Kobi!" Ye-Ye the distinguished designer shouted after me.
"I'll be there in a minute!" I yelled back.
I had to see what Ro was up to first...

When my toes touched the soft cool grains of dark sand, I looked up and stopped. All of a sudden, I knew what the flower was for. Or who, rather. There, lying stretched out on the beach was a seal. Only, it wasn't moving; it was just lying there, surrounded by a billion grains of sand. It was like the sand was trying to help it up. I watched Ro as he slowly scooped himself over to the lifeless creature, lowered his head and gently placed the flower on one of the dead animal's flippers. A strange feeling came into my throat. It was similar to the one I had on the day I realized Nai-Nai was never coming home. My throat also has a good memory. Or maybe sad things are just much easier to remember.

I thought about the seal the whole day. It's like when you accidentally let go of a balloon and it drifts off into the atmosphere. For hours, you think about where it's gone or about flying after it. I felt bad for teasing Ro about the flower. Ye-Ye and I should've known better.

I was so distracted that I couldn't concentrate on anything in school that day. Luckily the only consequence of this was that the science teacher, Mrs. Ouyang,[7] threw a blackboard eraser at me. When she saw that my mind was elsewhere, she suddenly asked me to define artificial intelligence. Of course, I was totally surprised to have a question directed at me, so I just said the first thing that popped into my head.

Unfortunately, the first thing that popped into my head was that artificial intelligence referred to 'people *pretending* to be clever.'[8]

Afterwards, Mrs. Ouyang said she'd merely thrown the eraser at me to demonstrate one or two basic laws of physics, but you didn't have to be not-pretending clever to know that it actually was because I wasn't paying attention. What she meant to say was that I was skating on thin ice[9] because I wasn't listening in class. For teachers, that's a sure sign of truant tendencies. They don't know about sand trying to help seals up and all that stuff. Still, I suppose she's right, if your mind goes wandering it's kind of the same as not really being present, because you're not really taking anything in. If your brain's not in class, then neither are you.

Fortunately there weren't any other incidents, but it was a really long day. My good friend Milkshake asked me several times what was wrong, but I didn't want to tell *him* about the seal. I didn't want him to feel sad as well. Sometimes seals and people leave and don't come back, and sometimes life has to stop. It didn't seem fair. You never know what's around the next corner, let alone where the corner is! That's why you should always have a flower ready, just in case.

After school, Ye-Ye and I dug a grave close to the banana
trees and blooming azaleas[10] on the far side of the yard. I
didn't have any nice clothes to wear so I wore my wetsuit.[11]
That was the blackest thing I could find. Ye-Ye wore his only
tie and jacket during the burial and looked very solemn. I think
Ye-Ye buried someone else that day, because he wasn't really
a sentimental guy and he was crying far too much about a seal
that he didn't know. After that, he never said any names in his
dreams anymore. We didn't surf that day.

"... just in case."

註解

1　片語：指某個人今天心情不好 'to wake up on the wrong side of the bed'

2　鰭狀肢 flipper (詞彙 flip)

3　便道，捷徑 shortcut (詞彙 shortcut=short+cut)

4　滑板 skateboard (詞彙 skateboard=skate+board)

5　衝浪板 surfboard (詞彙 surfboard=surf+board)

6　衝浪板線 surfboard leash

7　歐陽老師 literally Oūyáng Teacher (Oūyáng is a common two character surname)

8　artificial 有兩個意思：「人工」和「假的」。 答案應該是「人工智能」但是口筆脫口而說的是「有人在假裝很聰明」。

9　片語：談論 (或做) 易引起分歧 (或反對意見、其他麻煩) 的事，情況危急 , 如履薄冰 'to be skating on thin ice'

10　杜鵑花

11　防寒衣 (詞彙 wetsuit=wet+suit)

Rice

飯

Chapter **03** / Tuesday

Milkshake

I really hope I didn't make you cry in the last chapter either. I didn't mean to. I know sadness is contagious, so I try to avoid talking about it, but I just thought we had to get it out of the way as soon as possible. And I had to introduce you to Milkshake because he's my second best friend. Milkshake's the same age as me but he's very different. In fact, I don't think we have any similarities. He's been working at his mom's drink shop[1] since he was five (hence the nickname), so he's really good with money and talking and all that adult stuff. He already has two wallets, one briefcase, three bank accounts and shares in some silicon company. Oh, and he's started writing a book for kids on how to invest your pocket money. What a freak! Sometimes he even dresses like an economist and listens to jazz music. One day, Milkshake's going to be the Minister of Economics and establish drink shops of his own, that's for sure. They'll be setting up websites about him.

Unfortunately, in-between homework, exams, comics, accumulating his personal savings, worrying about global economics and pouring pearl milk teas, he doesn't get much time to hang out with me in the afternoons. But, when we do get together, we always have loads of fun. Milkshake's a fun guy...when he's not talking about money, of course.

"Hey, guess what, Kobi! I invented a new flavor yesterday."
Since Milkshake thinks of his drink shop as more of a
laboratory, I wasn't really surprised to hear this. However,
I was still curious to know what the new flavor was.
"Cool! What is it, Shakes?"
"Take a guess!" He snapped his fingers once or twice to
hurry me up.
My face went as blank as my mind.
"Oh, never mind," he continued impatiently, "you're too slow.
The new flavor is...taro[2] and ginger milk tea!"
Milkshake announced his new flavor with great pride and
confidence. Almost as if he'd invented an amazing new time
machine or something.
"Mmm," I replied. "Sounds good."
"Good? Just *good*?" asked an astonished Milkshake.

Well, he pretended to be astonished, but I think he knew
all along that he wasn't going to get any enthusiastic
responses or worthwhile feedback from me. He also knew
that he'd have to teach me a thing or two about flavors and
would have to shoulder the burden of improving my taste
in... um... tastes.
"Kobi, I don't want to sound critical or anything, but you
really are very ignorant when it comes to flavoring things,

aren't you?"

I was still trying to figure out how this rhetorical question might not be interpreted as criticism, when Milkshake continued.

"Let me guess, Kobi...You think, for example, that vanilla is the best flavor ever discovered. Or that ketchup and cheese are the best complements for any dish on earth. In fact, you probably would shove anything remotely edible down your throat, wouldn't you?"

Before I could deny the ignorance or the bias or the appetite, he continued.

"You would never dream of combining almond and red bean, would you? Or walnut and apple for that matter. For you, dipping anything in sugar would be an improvement, right? Ha! If I told you to drizzle some vinegar over your ice cream, you'd probably wet your pants!"

He shook his head as if he was deeply disappointed.

"It really is a pity that you can't truly appreciate my talent and expertise, Ko my man. In a way, I pity you. In fact, it's tragic."

"T...T...T...Tragic?" I stammered.

"And I'll tell you what else is tragic, Kobi." he went on. "The fact that I have to blow my own trumpet[3] about it, now *that's* tragic. Praising oneself is lonesome. And such a bore!"

Milkshake the ambitious flavor magician and future backbone of the local economy was right, I really didn't know much about flavors. I tried to look embarrassed so as not to give Milkshake the impression that flavors were unimportant to me.
I scratched my knee for a while before asking, "How do you do it, Milkshake?"
"Do what?"
"You know. How do you come up with important...I mean delicious new flavors all the time?"

Milkshake looked far off into the horizon as if he was seriously wondering if he could share his secret with me. Of course, secretly he'd been looking forward to telling me all day.
"Promise not to mention this to anyone?"
"I promise! Not a soul."
When he'd waited long enough to make sure I really truly did desire to know, Milkshake rubbed his chin like all intelligent people do and went ahead with the disclosure.
"Well, you see, Kobi, all great inventors need some kind of inspiration. A kind of philosopher's stone.[4] Without inspiration, even the best inventor would never amount to

very much."

"An inspirational stone?"

I liked the way the word 'inspirational' sounded when I said it. Like even just the sound of the word was enough to magically invent something all on its own.

"Yep, inventors require something that inspires them to think differently from other people, so they can turn ordinary things into extraordinary things. It's called innovation. If some special humans—like myself—didn't specialize in being inspired, the human race would've been extinct long ago. In fact, the only reason you exist at all, is because people like me are so innovative."

Milkshake was looking wiser and wiser (and more and more special) as he spoke. I think he knew he was.

"The truth is, Kobi, if you can find your inspiration, even *you* can invent something."

I too looked far into the horizon searching for my inspiration, but all I could see was a large red and white ship moving very slowly in the direction of Keelung.[5]

"So...what inspires you?" I asked, genuinely curious.

Milkshake looked at me for a while very seriously, before I saw his lips breaking into a smile. There was a gleam in his innovative eye.

"Rice," he whispered.

"Rice?" This time I was surprised.

"Yep," he said calmly, "rice. You do know what rice is, don't you? Or have I underestimated your ignorance?"

I was too surprised to even nod.

"Rice," he repeated, this time in English. "R-I-C-E. Please tell me you don't think it's the plural of 'rouse'."[6]

"I know, I know, Milkshake," I said finally. "I know what rice is. Rice, as in excellent-source-of-starch, that rice. But..."

"You see, Kobi, every day when I open my lunchbox, I look at my rice very carefully. You'd be amazed at how many different shapes and patterns you can see in it if you look hard enough. In fact, it's just like the clouds."

He pointed to the sky without looking up.

The temptation was too strong and I glanced up at the sky—even though I know how silly I looked doing it—especially since his eyes hadn't raised an inch.

Milkshake, with a tolerant smile, continued.

"Today I saw a fat little taro and a slice of ginger lying in my rice. The perfect blend of texture and spice. It was a massive discovery. I didn't even have to test my theory, Kobi. Right away, I knew it was promising."

I sat for a while very quietly, reflecting on this sensational dialogue. (Many adults make the assumption that adolescents have a definite dislike for reflection, but this is certainly not true. We love to reflect.) I glimpsed over at Milkshake the flavor wizard. He was doing some reflecting of his own. Secretly, I studied his face like immigration officers study passports in the movies. Was he pulling my leg[7] or something? After a while I realized that he was actually quite serious about the relationship between carbohydrates and creativity, so the last thing I wanted to do was say something stupid. "But, Shakes...What if you have noodles for lunch?"

When he heard this question, Milkshake laughed out loud until his coconut-shaped head shook like a rattle. I wasn't quite sure what he was thinking, so I burst out laughing too. Of course, I never questioned his authority on the subject again, but I promised myself to look into it when I had a chance.

I think Ye-Ye's inspiration comes from yam leaves, but I did catch him once or twice looking very carefully at the white spots on Ro-Ro Gway-Gway's back. I wonder if those can turn into flavors as well...

"Please tell me ʊ don't think it's the plural of rouse."

Milkshake's "rice" dreams.

註解

1　飲料店 'drink shop' here refers to an informal tea house, consisting of perhaps just two or three tables and a small stand or counter where customers can buy all kinds of tea drinks

2　芋頭 taro

3　片語：吹牛 *'to blow one's own trumpet'*, to brag or boast

4　魔法石，點金石 A legendary substance thought by alchemists to have the power to transform ordinary base metals into gold

5　基隆 Keelung, large port and city situated on the north coast of Taiwan

6　'rouse' 其實平常有弄醒 / 叫醒或激起 (情感等) / 激怒 / 使激動 / 驚起 / 喚起 / 使覺醒的意思。Milkshake 是開 Kobi 的玩笑說他那麼笨認為 rice 跟 mice (mouse 的複數) 一樣是 rouse 的複數。

7　片語：耍弄或取笑某人 *'to be pulling someone's leg'*

Water

水

Chapter **04** / Wednesday. Thursday
Friday. Saturday

Control

Ro mourned the seal's death for a full five days. This was
the longest I'd seen him stay away from the ocean. I don't
know if he knew the seal personally or if he was just missing
someone else instead, but I could tell that the whole thing
really depressed him. Ro has an awesome lung capacity so
he can easily dive to depths of over a thousand meters (an
amazing achievement in itself), but somehow this was the
lowest he'd ever been. Lower than any of those underwater
canyons or valleys he explored. Emotionally low. Okay, I
don't know if turtles really do get depressed or emotionally
low but—trust me—he wasn't himself for a while.

That's why the sixth morning after the seal's appearance
was such a relief. At sunrise,[1] Ro slid swiftly down the
tree-trunk shortcut to the beach. He was in the waves in a
flash. I'd been watching him for a full fifteen minutes while
I was sorting laundry and daydreaming about Ting-Ting,[2] so
as soon as he started to move, I ran to grab my board wax.[3]
(Oh, Ting-Ting's the girl from the fruit store by the way.
The girl I'm too terrified to talk to.) By the time I'd changed
into my wetsuit and reached the beach, Ro was already
riding his third or fourth wave of the morning. He's a bit like
the tortoise in that fable[4] —somehow he always gets to the
water before me.

"...somehow, he always gets to the water before me."

Surfing at daybreak is my favorite. It heals anything.
Depression, stress, being orphaned because somewhere
else is awesome, not being able to talk to the girl you like
etc. Anything. It's the ultimate cure. I quickly paddled out to
join him, laughing excitedly as I got closer and closer. It was
wonderful to taste and smell the salty water again. Five
days is a really long time, especially if they're mournful. I
sure hope no other seals turn up. Unless they're breathing
of course.

It was a beautiful March morning, dry and sunny. The
sea across the bay was glistening like a crystal ball. How
could a liquid mixture of just hydrogen, oxygen and salt be

so majestic? It's a miracle. A miracle of chemistry. The temperature of the water was a bit low but I couldn't think of a better way to wake up in the mornings. Cold water makes you feel alive.

I think about Ting-Ting often to be honest, but you can't tell her that. Under no circumstances can you tell her that. Ye-Ye and I love eating fruit so I have to go there at least twice a week. I don't plan on dying of embarrassment twice a week as well, which is what will happen if you tell her. I wouldn't be able to face her. For now, let's just keep it a secret. Sure, most seasonal fruits are available at one or two other fruit shops in town, but Ting-Ting's has the juiciest sweetsops[5] and strawberries in the winter (Ye-Ye's favorites) and the sweetest watermelon and cherries in the summer (Kobi's favorites), so I don't really have an alternative. I don't know why I think about her. I'm not sure if I like her, or if I just like the way she smiles.

Milkshake says she smiles at all the customers, just like he does at the drink shop. Not because she particularly likes any of them, but because it makes economic sense to smile. He's got a good point, but I don't think *all* the customers daydream about her when she smiles at *them*. Or about him for that matter. I certainly don't daydream about the scallion cake[6] lady either, and she's smiled at me a million times.

"Ting-Ting? She's not even *tha-a-t* pretty, Ko." Milkshake looked away when he made this remark. It was the longest 'that' I'd ever heard.

I started thinking that maybe love was clouding my judgment. Ye-Ye says it's impossible to control what we think about by thinking. It's like trying to waterproof a tennis racket with a second racket. It just can't be done. So, he maintains, we shouldn't even try. Rather, we should stop thinking altogether. Ye-Ye forgot to tell me that it's not so easy to not try.

Wow, Ro was really enjoying himself this morning! There he was, catching wave after wave, riding, twisting, turning and splashing like a dolphin in love with a mermaid. I'd never seen him having so much fun. I knew Ro; he wasn't showing off,[7] he was just happy. Happy and free. Every time he was on a wave it looked like the two of them had been the best of friends for centuries. Not only best of friends, but also two necessary halves of one whole, unbreakable something. Neither was trying to control or dominate the other. They weren't competing with each other either. They were just flowing alongside one another. It was a beautiful alliance. I was jealous. I tried to control my jealousy. I couldn't. Then I tried to stop thinking about the jealousy, but I couldn't do that either.

I bet Ro doesn't try to control his thoughts.

註解

1　日出 (詞彙 sunrise=sun+rise)
2　婷婷 Chinese girls' name meaning 'graceful'
3　(抹在衝浪板上的) 板蠟 board wax
4　龜兔賽跑 The Tortoise & the Hare, 伊索寓言 Aesop's Fables
5　釋迦 sweetsop
6　蔥油餅 green onion or scallion cake (詞彙 green, onion, cake)
7　片語：炫耀 'to show off'

Love

愛

Chapter 05 / Sunday. Monday

The Heart Sings (Too Loudly)

The Heart Sings (Too Loudly)

There comes a time in every young man's life when he has to be embarrassed in front of his friends. When he wants to climb into a hollow in the ground far away from everyone's mocking gaze and never come out. For Milkshake, that day had arrived.

I'd overslept and was late for school. This meant I had to take a shortcut through Mr. Wu's[1] back garden to save some precious time. Desperate times call for desperate measures. He'd kill me if he saw me, of course, but it was the only option I had at the time. Little did I know that it would lead to a sequence of bizarre events over the next few weeks...

Unfortunately, quite by chance, Mr. Wu had also overslept that morning. His entire morning routine had been disrupted. As a result, he just happened to be doing some Tai Ji shadow boxing[2] in his garden at that very moment. The retired engineer's movements were very elegant. He had just rhythmically placed a large imaginary watermelon on a small imaginary table beside his right knee,[3] when he looked up and spotted me. I was tiptoeing with great speed past his favorite orchids.[4]
Now, when Ye-Ye makes me do Tai Ji with him I have to pretend to be really focused and ignore everything else around me. Otherwise, Ye-Ye—who's also supposed

"...it turned out he was a pretender too."

to be focused and ignoring everything else—will notice immediately. I know you're actually supposed to be far away in Tai Ji Land when you're doing it. Watermelon, watermelon, far away. Table, table far away. Tai-Ji Land. To be honest, I was hoping that's where Mr. Wu would be when we suddenly made eye contact. Unfortunately, it turned out that he was a pretender too.

"And where do you think you're going, you stinky little ghost?!" I knew he was going to say something before he actually did, but the threatening question still startled me. I think my blood actually froze. This wasn't good. Mr. Wu had warned me before about running through his garden. This time I knew that if he caught me, he was going to slice me up into tiny pieces with his kitchen knife made from Jinmen bombshells.[5] I could hear it in his operatic voice.

"Come here you little monster! I'm going to crack every stinking bone in your body, boil your blood, hang you from my brick balcony and then bury you in the shallow bog behind us!"

The stout, barefoot little man was furious. He was so furious that I thought he would have to be hospitalized. He had warned me too many times before. This was the last straw. Plus, he wasn't really famous for his eloquence either, so I'm sure having to say so many *b*'s in one sentence just made it worse. He rushed toward me with his hands stretched out in front of him snarling like a wild bear. He was ready for battle. He was ready to tear me to pieces. His cheeks were shaking like jelly after an earthquake. I was almost certain he was going to erupt like a volcano.

Despite all this, I found myself being quite rational. I was thinking like Sherlock Holmes.[6] Judging from the way he shadow boxed, I knew Mr. Wu probably wouldn't be able to crack *every* bone in my body. Maybe just fifty or sixty. I therefore concluded that I'd probably survive the fiery eruption. However, there was still no doubt that he was strong enough to make me suffer unimaginable pain. No one likes pain, not even Sherlock. In the end, I decided that the best would be to just bolt for safety. Considering the situation, it was still by far the most sensible thing to do.

In a flash, I skipped over his carrots and his cabbage patch. A long "Soooorrrrrryyyyyyyy!" (in the local dialect)[7] followed me all the way as I sprinted down the road like a rabbit. I turned around once just in time to see a purple eggplant,[8] and then an onion, flying in my direction. I was under attack. Weapons of mass digestion.[9] Mr. Wu had launched one last guerrilla style assault!

Luckily, my schoolbag shielded me from the edible missiles— it was raining vegetables! I dodged this way and that before finally disappearing around the corner. The bear with the wobbly cheeks didn't chase me. I was safe for the moment. However, I knew I'd have to watch my back from now on. There was nothing wrong with Mr. Wu's memory either, so he was sure to have his revenge at some point. Terrific! Now I had to worry about that *and* about being late for school. Speaking of which, the bell had just rung.

About fifty meters from the school gate I slowed down. A large group of students, with a few teachers in-

The Heart Sings (Too Loudly)

"Weapon of mass digestion."

between, had herded together like cattle in the middle of the front lawn. They seemed to have crowded around something lying on the ground right under the national flag. The rest of the children and the teachers had already made their way to class after the morning's assembly. That's very strange, I thought to myself, as I tiptoed a few meters closer and hid behind an old banyan tree.[10] Most of the cattle—I mean kids—were giggling and chatting non-stop. The handful of teachers were trying to look serious and settle them down. It was like everyone had gathered for a royal aboriginal wedding or something. With every pair of eyes concentrating on the center of the circle, I decided to take a chance on joining the rest of the group without being noticed. Keeping low, I silently snuck through the gate and blended with the outer ring of pupils facing the main school building.

When I caught my breath and was sure that no one had seen me, I popped up like toast in a toaster. None of the children or teachers assembled on the lawn paid any attention whatsoever to the toast. I gave a sigh of relief. Then I gave the chubby little seventh grader next to me a poke in the ribs with my elbow. (I don't really like it when people elbow *me* in the ribs, so I guess that makes me a bit of a hypocrite, but I just couldn't contain my curiosity.)

"Hey, dude, what happened?" I asked once he finally tore his eyes away from the main focal point to look at the rib poker.

"Some ninth grader fainted during the anthem!" he spat out excitedly through his braces. It was like he was attending a rock concert or something.

I could see that he was extremely pleased to pass on the fact that someone had passed out. That someone had provided an unexpected source of entertainment. He sounded like a parrot and looked like a koala bear with acne but there was no time to explore such an interesting phenomenon.

"Which ninth grader?" I asked.

I tried to think which of the boys and girls in my class were potential fainters.

"The guy from the drink shop!" the girl next to him whispered impatiently, unable to hold out any longer.

(There's a lot of reflecting during adolescence, but that

doesn't necessarily mean that we have time for patience.)
"You know, the one with the big nose and the pineapple
hairstyle," she added.
An image of Milkshake the drink magician flashed before my
eyes.
"Why's there soil all over your bag?" inquired the koala bear
suddenly. "And why do you smell like onions?"
On second thought, it sounded more like an accusation than
an inquiry.

I had already been bombarded with vegetables this morning, so
I wasn't going to hang around to be bombarded by questions as
well. Instead, I just smiled mysteriously and tried to get a little
closer. Was it really him who had fainted? Surely not... With a
push and a shove, I eventually gained access to the inner ring of
the youthful gathering. It was at that point that I first saw the big
sharp nose of my second best friend Milkshake pointing straight
up to the heavens. The toes of his well-polished school shoes
were pointing in the same direction.
Kneeling on the grass beside him was Mr. C.O. Ma.¹¹ No one
knows what the initials stand for but he's our Biology teacher.
He's a fine athlete too. In fact, he's a local ping-pong champion.
He's won the county table tennis championship eight times in a
row now. Last year he beat himself in the final because nobody

dared to play against him.

"Shakes!" I shouted as I dropped down to his side before I could stop myself. "Shakes, what's wrong!?"

"It's okay, my boy," said Mr. Ma calmly as he turned his shiny, bald head towards me. "Wang Qing Jun[12] has merely fainted. Give him some room so he can recover. He needs to breathe fresh air. I don't think giving off a nasty smell of onions and screaming at him will be very helpful."

"Yes, Sir."

Still pondering this unexpected diagnosis, I forced myself to follow Mr. Ma's instructions and retreated a little. I was so deep in thought that it took me a while before I finally felt the hand on my left shoulder. I turned to see Little Shu[13] standing next to me fiddling with her ponytail. Her eyes were as big as lychees.[14]

Little Shu had a broad forehead and eyelashes like a giraffe. Since kindergarten, she's always had the best report card in class. Calligraphy, Science, Math, English, you name it. That girl's just unbeatable.[15] In fact, the only thing I can *almost* match her in is PE![16] Anyway, she's always had the best grades because she can convert Celsius[17] into Fahrenheit and memorize geographical data like the average annual rainfall in Yunlin County.[18] And because she's the kind of person who somehow knows that MRT stands for 'Mass Rapid Transit'. And that bats are the only mammals that can fly. And the reasons for the collapse of the Mongol Empire. Oh, and the common symptoms of pneumonia. And the fact that pounds used to equal 20 shillings but are now made up of a hundred pennies. You get the picture. Little Shu had a big brain under that broad forehead somewhere.

More importantly, Little Shu with the big brain usually knew what was going on outside the classroom as well. Anytime something happened, Little Shu was there. She could be relied on for all relevant event descriptions and updates. She's going to make a great private investigator one day. Or she's going to work for the Central Weather Bureau.

"What happened, Shu Mei?"[19] I asked, still in disbelief.

"I don't know, Kobi," she replied. "All I know is, when we got to the 'one heart, one virtue' part,[20] Qing Jun just collapsed like a sack of pumpkins!"

"Shh, shh, shh! He's coming 'round," said Mr. Ma suddenly. He raised his one hand to the heavens for silence. It was as if he was about to recite a sermon or make the biggest purchase of his life at an auction. His other hand was busying itself with fanning Milkshake's face with a ping-pong paddle. (The latter had been produced from his back trouser pocket. For Mr. Ma, a ping-pong paddle was as indispensable as a mobile phone.)

"Quiet, everyone!" he finally said, still fanning. All the murmurs and whispers were slowly dying down. "I think he's trying to say something."

Immediately, there was complete silence in the circle of curious children. The unconscious[21] boy's audience was anticipating something remarkable. Something very memorable. Cellphone cameras were on standby to capture the moment forever. (Apart from Ro, there's not much to photograph in the countryside, you know.) We all leaned forward and tried to get as close as possible without falling over.

I fixed my gaze on Milkshake's intelligent face. His eyes were closed but I can affirm that his lips were definitely moving. That's all that was moving. We waited. Suddenly, like a flash of lightning, he stretched out a hand and grabbed Mr. Ma's orange-striped necktie. Mr. Ma's head was violently pulled forward, much to the enjoyment of all the spectators. Their noses were almost touching. This was the most entertaining morning we'd had at school for

years. I think if everyone wasn't so curious to see what was
going to happen next, they probably would have given the
two of them a big hand! It got better...

Still not fully conscious, Milkshake gave one or two tugs
on the tie. Mr. Ma slowly raised himself up a little off the
ground. Milkshake's upper body followed, as if attached
by a rope. Mr. Ma's starched white collar was rising up
too. Milkshake's eyes were still shut tight, but I could
swear there was a smile on his pale face. The Ping-Pong
champion was being strangled a little bit but he's got a
pretty good sense of humor, so I'm sure he saw the funny
side of things as well. Then there was a long pause as we
waited for the smiling, suspended Milkshake to say what he
wanted to say. Silence. Anticipation...

Finally, we heard a very faint, hoarse sound escaping from
Milkshake's dry lips: "Ting-Ting...Ting-Ting...Ting-Ting...I...
I...I adore you."

註 解

1　吳先生 literally Wú Mister. Wú was one of the Three Kingdoms into which China was divided between 220 and 256 AD. Today it is a common Chinese surname.

2　太極拳 shadow boxing, Tai Chi, Taiji, T'aichi (詞彙 shadow, boxing)

3　吳先生打太極拳時動作很像從空中拿著一顆圓圓的大西瓜，抱起來後放在他腳下 Mr. Wu's elegant Tai Ji movements resemble that of someone placing their arms around a large round watermelon in a wide circular motion, gathering it up and then placing it neatly down on a small table situated next their lower leg, as denoted by slowly joining the hands in front of the lower legs.

4　蘭花 orchid

5　用炸彈殼做的金門菜刀, 詞彙 bombshell (炸彈殼)=bomb+shell; Jinmen (金門), literally Golden Gate or Golden Door, is the name given to group of Taiwanese islands situated to the northwest of the main island of Taiwan. Having been the site of an important naval base during the Chinese civil war between the National Party (KMT) and Communist Party, the islands are today known for their high quality kitchen knives (菜刀) produced using metal obtained from empty bombshells and for their renowned sorghum liquor (高粱酒).

6　福爾摩斯 Sherlock Holmes

7　歹勢 (pronounced pǎisei in Taiwanese)

8　茄子 (詞彙 eggplant=egg+plant)

9　大規模消化性武器（原本為 weapons of mass destruction 大規模殺傷性武器）

10　榕樹

11　coma 昏睡 (狀態)；昏迷 Mǎ, literally 'horse', a common family name.

12　王青俊 Boys' name. Wáng (王) is a common surname meaning 'king'. The word 'qīng' (青) can mean blue or green, while jùn (俊) means handsome.

The Heart Sings (Too Loudly)

13 小淑 literally Little Shū. Shū (淑) is commonly used in girls'
names and is usually said of a woman who is refined, pure,
virtuous or beautiful. Xiǎo (小), meaning 'small' or 'little', is
commonly added for diminutive name forms.

14 荔枝 also 'litchi'

15 無敵的 (詞彙 unbeatable=un (否定的) +beat+able; 參考
unbelievable, unimaginable)

16 體育課 Physical Education

17 攝氏 also 'Centigrade'

18 雲林縣 literally 'Cloud Forest County' ; county situated on
the west coast of Taiwan

19 淑美 Kobi addresses her using her full name instead of the
diminutive Little Shu.

20 國歌裡面的 「一心，一德」部分。This refers to a line in the
Taiwanese national anthem.

21 不省人事，失去知覺 (詞彙 unconscious=un (否定
的) +conscious)

Book

書

Chapter 06 / ☀ Tuesday

Bananas, Books and Bones

Bananas, Books and Bones

Have I mentioned before that my surfboard is painted like
a banana? I don't think I did. Brother Liao[1] from the old
surf shop up the road helped me paint it. Brother Liao's
quite a character. He thinks he can do anything. He's very
proud of being one quarter aborigine and tells everyone that
he's descended from a long line of chiefs. He has a 'Son
of Chiefs' tattoo on his left calf muscle just in case some
people don't believe him. He also has a pet parrot, Mr. Beak,
that he talks to for hours and a pet kitten, Mr. Claw, that
he completely ignores.

Okay, he's a bit weird but I get along well with Brother Liao.
To be honest, he's a bit of a drunk too (his three favorite
words are 'down the hatch!'[2]) and he's certainly no Picasso,[3]
but the banana board he designed for me is by far my most
valuable possession. That and my illustrated book about
marine animals. The librarian, Auntie Guo,[4] gave that to
me last autumn for helping her clean the library basement.
That book more than doubled my vocabulary. I like books,
by the way, especially the ones with illustrations. They're
so much better than computers. Books never beep. Or run
out of battery power. Sometimes, if I ask nicely, Mr. Ma, a
strict but reasonable man, will lend me some of the biology
textbooks in his office. Apart from classifying virtually the

"Along with the book about marine animals, my most valuable possession."

entire animal kingdom (what could be cooler than animals!?), they also help to combat boredom. And to take my mind off bad weather, dead seals and one of my best friends being in love with the girl I have a crush on. She's not even *that* pretty.

Anyway, I take good care of my books and my banana board. And Ro of course. Ro's probably the easiest 'cause he kind of takes care of himself. Ye-Ye says he's easily the best guest he's ever had and he's had more than he can remember. That's right, we regard Ro more as a family guest or family member than a pet. Sometimes he'll go away for long periods of time, but he always comes back. He always comes home.

According to my *Illustrated Guide to Marine Animals*, leatherbacks are the biggest turtles in the world. They grow up to two meters in length. They also cover the greatest distances when they're swimming around the planet hunting for jellyfish and looking for company. The Gulf of Mexico,[5] the Cape of Good Hope,[6] the Great Barrier Reef,[7] I bet Ro's seen it all. I'm not sure if he's crossed every latitude, but I'm almost positive that he's passed every longitude. I think he's read the *Illustrated Guide to Marine Animals* too because he's only one meter long and he still thinks he's the biggest turtle alive. He's not afraid of anything. Storms, cold, sharks, he doesn't fear any of these. He knows he can weather any storm or any beast that Nature could throw at him. Not even typhoons scare him. Not even alligators scare him. Okay, I've never actually seen him around alligators but I'm sure they wouldn't scare him one little bit either. He's too smart for them.

I know he can take care of himself on his travels but there's just one thing that makes me nervous. Plastic bags. Mankind's most dangerous invention. Ever. Humans throw plastic bags in the sea and sometimes Ro and his siblings think they're jellyfish. It's shocking really. He's a clever turtle and he's quite picky when it comes to food, so he'll probably spit them out, but I'm really a bit fearful that one day he won't be able to in time. I almost can't breathe either when I think about that. If you see a human throwing a plastic bag in the sea and leaving local ecosystems in ruins, please phone Mr. Wu and tell him to go and set them straight.

In case you're thinking that's what I wanted to do to Milkshake...it's definitely not, by the way. Okay, I had underestimated how much he liked Ting-Ting. I admit that. He adored her so much that he collapsed under the national flag. It just shows you, emotions are like icebergs. And what never surfaces is much more than what you actually see. This was serious.

But still, I was optimistic. The way I saw it was: when you work around so many different flavors on a daily basis, as Milkshake does, you probably like new ones better all the time. So, all I had to do was to wait a few days until he got bored and decided to like someone else. A new flavor. Basically, I just had to wait for the iceberg to melt. Then, I could tell him that it was my turn to adore Ting-Ting and all would be back to normal. Surely that was a very logical conclusion. A slight delay in the plans, that's all it was. Not really that serious. In fact, I could even imagine the three of us laughing together about it some day.

Turns out I was a little bit wrong about this as well but we'll get to that. Optimists who are in love are often wrong. We'll also get to how Brother Liao saved Ye-Ye's life one day when he was riding the wrong scooter up the wrong alley. I mean Brother Liao was on the wrong scooter and in the wrong alley, not Ye-Ye. How did this happen? Well, it's quite a long story, but let me just say for now that it had a lot to do with the flaws in Brother Liao's character. For one thing, he was notorious for napping whenever he could, regardless of the time of day. This was not his only bad habit. Like that pig in the story about the monk and the monkey,[8] he had many. These included being addicted to betel nuts,[9] Long Life Cigarettes and TV.

However, by far his worst and most dangerous habit was that of sometimes getting very drunk, falling asleep and then riding scooters. I mean riding scooters in his sleep. Oh, and they were never his own scooters. *Other* people's scooters! Needless to say, this made everyone in the town a little nervous about being anywhere other than on their own scooters. Almost as nervous as the fact that Brother Liao found all pajamas to be as itchy as chickenpox and often preferred to sleep naked.

Now, if his riding or his figure were as good as his painting, there wouldn't have been much of a safety issue. But, unfortunately being around Brother Liao was dangerous enough when he was as sober as a judge and had his eyes open. And his clothes on. Amazingly enough, however, nothing too serious had ever happened on one of Brother Liao's naked scooter naps. Sure, he had a few scars here and there (in places people normally don't have scars), but how he never fatally injured himself or anyone else with his reckless conduct—not to mention cause serious damage to

"Other people's scooters!"

the entire neighborhood—no one knows. Just as well, because no one would dare dream of selling him any insurance. Some said it was a miracle that nothing horrible ever happened. Brother Liao said it's because he's one quarter aborigine and can do anything.

Anyway, I can hear you thinking: why did I want my surfboard to look like a banana? That's easy. Bananas are my favorite fruit, after watermelons and cherries in the summer, of course. In fact, Ye-Ye and I eat bananas every day. We even shred the peels up to make a fertilizer, so the lilies and roses in our flower garden eat bananas every day as well. Now you know. That's why I wanted a banana surfboard. Besides, a surfboard shaped like a cherry or a watermelon (or a star fruit[10] or a wax apple[11] or whatever) would be very difficult to ride without embarrassing yourself in front of all the girls in bikinis[12] on the beach. Nearly as difficult as riding someone else's scooter in your sleep, naked and drunk.

| 註 解 |

1 廖哥 Lìao is a common family name, while Gē (哥 meaning 'older brother') is commonly used in older male names as a respectful, yet less formal, form of address.

2 乾杯！iterally 'dry glass'; also 'Cheers!'

3 畢卡索 Pablo Picasso

4 郭阿姨 literally Guō Aunt; Guō is a common family name.

5 墨西哥灣 literally 'ink west older brother bay'

6 好望角 literally 'good hope horn'

7 大堡礁 literally 'large fort reef'

8 豬八戒 literally 'pig eight quit'; pig-like character in the famous Chinese novel Journey to the West (西遊記) famous for his many vices

9 檳榔 mild stimulant often chewed wrapped in betel leaves; also Areca nut

10 楊桃 literally 'poplar peach'; also carambola (詞彙 star, fruit)

11 蓮霧 literally 'lotus fog' (詞彙 bell, fruit)

12 比基尼 bikini (外來語 loanword)

Dragon

龍

Chapter 07 / Wednesday. Thursday

Dragons

This morning, the school principal Mrs. Wang [1] (she has a head shaped like a papaya and usually wears too much lipstick) announced that the Dragon Boat Festival was coming up in a couple months' time. She said the children who wanted to join a rowing team and take part in the annual races, had to meet her husband Mr. Wang after school at the tennis court.

That might sound like a simple announcement but there's something you have to know about Mr. Wang. He's a former military commander. Now he's a local police officer. And, he's the husband of a school principal who is even more bossy than he is. You didn't want to mess with Mr. Wang. We all knew that, but Mrs. Wang repeated it several times this morning just in case.

She put a lot of emphasis on the fact that her spouse had a violent temper. And that he could not—ever ever (yes, she said ever twice)—tolerate bad behavior. She said if you looked in the dictionary for the definition of 'punishment', there would be nothing but a picture of her husband in his dark blue police uniform. And he wouldn't be smiling. He never smiles. After this, she took four and a quarter minutes highlighting exactly how little mercy he had and how much he hated children. Finally, to sum up, she warned us that if

any noisy volunteers were going there just to fool around,
Mr. Wang would probably shoot them with his police pistol.
Or give them twenty lashes with his whip. Or drown them in
the river like the Warring States imperial advisor and poet
who started the whole thing.[2] Or, worst of all, even call off
the whole festival. By the time she had finished announcing,
emphasizing and warning, the entire microphone was full of
lipstick.

Once my fear had subsided, my Sherlock brain was back. I
battled to understand what a cop or a tennis court could
teach me about extracurricular rowing. To be honest, I also
couldn't understand how canceling a festival was worse than
being shot, whipped or drowned. Apart from that though,
my brain and I were both bursting with excitement. I was like
a pickpocket in a train station! This is one of my favorite
times of the year. One of the highlights of my lunar calendar.
Whoever had the novel idea of racing in colorful dragon-like
canoes down a river because someone drowned themselves
was a real genius. As far as I'm concerned, anyone who is
opposed to the idea must be out of their minds!

Ye-Ye told me that my father used to love watching the
races. He said that's where my parents met. Ye-Ye says one

day I too will meet a girl in a place with dragons and that's the girl I'm going to marry. He says it's a family tradition. He says the tradition dates back to the early 18th century. Just between you and me, Nai-Nai told me that she and Ye-Ye met when he helped to remove a chameleon[3] from her shoulder in the park. A chameleon? Now, I don't think that really counts, do you? I mean, it's not like lobsters,[4] dragonflies, tornadoes[5] or dinosaurs[6] would count, now would they?

Besides, I don't remember any dragons of any kind being around on the day I met Ting-Ting, and she's definitely the girl I'm going to marry. How on Earth could Ye-Ye explain the universe making an error like that? Instead, the universe decided...

Now, I don't like telling people this but I guess we've known each other for a few chapters already, so I'll just spit it out. But don't laugh. It's humiliating.

Instead, the universe decided that it would be better if we met in front of the toilet paper section of the local supermarket. The toilet paper aisle. You heard me – not in the chocolate aisle or the wrapping paper aisle, or even in the fake flower

Dragons

aisle. Nothing romantic like that. No, no, it had to be the toilet paper aisle. Now how, in the name of romance, can you possibly be a romantic about that kind of venue? I'm no expert but if you ask me, it's probably the most unromantic place ever. And definitely not somewhere you'd want to meet your future bride! When it comes to falling in love, toilet paper creates a powerful antigravity[7] field. Thanks for nothing, universe.

The only thing I can hope for is that Ting-Ting doesn't remember any of the details. Luckily, we were only five or six at the time. Fate can be quite cruel, as we've seen in the previous chapters, so it'll probably figure out a way to remind her. I'll just have to keep my fingers crossed that it doesn't. As for Ye-Ye, I'll just make up some story about there having been some gentian violet[8] or Styrofoam[9] boxes nearby at the time. If chameleons count, so do those.

Of course, I haven't told Ting-Ting any of this destiny or tradition stuff yet. I'm sure there'll be a right time and place for that, too, somewhere down the line. For now, I'll just stare at her when she's not looking. And dream of holding her hand. And contemplate writing an anonymous love letter or a poem summarizing my affection for her. (Would I ever have the courage to post it?!) Until then I'll just wait for the universe to do the rest. It'll hurt, but I'll just have to wait. By the way, why does romance have to be so painful anyway? Waiting for someone to realize that they like you (and that they're going to marry you) can be absolute torture if you ask me. Like having your feet tickled with some farmyard[10] fowl's feather.

Dearest Ting-Ting,
You make my heart sing.
When you smile at me,
It's like being in the sea
Where I don't have to think about thinking.

I didn't really know Officer Wang[11] personally, I have to confess. Most villagers are in agreement that he loves school reunions and those sorts of things. They say it gives him an excuse to talk about himself. It's also common knowledge that he hates his relatives because they deprive him of an opportunity to talk about himself at all costs. I admit, I'm not immune to public opinion and gossip, but I try not to let it make me too prejudiced. Ye-Ye says if there's anything in life one should avoid, it's prejudice. He says it's like a poison. A poison affects your senses. He says you can tell from just looking at prejudiced people that they have been poisoned.

My senses tell me that Officer Wang is very tall and skinny like a pharaoh or a pole, and has ears like a chimpanzee. I've also heard reports that his favorite hobby is boasting about bringing the crime rate in the village down to zero. He also loves fining Mr. Wu for parking his rusty Suzuki[12] jeep on the red line outside his own house. Officer Wang takes his occupation extremely seriously. Punishing violators of parking laws is his specialty, especially if it's Mr. Wu and his rusty vehicle that are responsible for the violation. In that case, Mr. Wang has the eyes of an eagle.

To be honest, nobody knows why he loves targeting the shadow boxer so much. I have a suspicion that good old prejudice might have something to do with it.

All in all, I wasn't sure how much the arrogant champion of law enforcement knew about dragon boat racing. But, I was still excited nevertheless. Ye-Ye would be super proud of me if I could make the school's rowing team. He'd love that. Then he could come and watch me and think about my father. I was also under the illusion that if I was part of the dragon boat crew, Ting-Ting would automatically fall in love with me and become my fireproof phoenix.[13]

Dragons really are useful. Even if you're not superstitious.

註 解

1　王校長 literally 'Wáng Principal'

2　屈原 This refers to the famous poet, Qu Yuan (340 – 278 BC), who is said to have drowned himself in a river and in whose memory the traditions of the Dragon Boat Festival are upheld.

3　變色龍 literally 'change color dragon'

4　龍蝦 literally 'dragon shrimp'

5　龍捲風 literally 'dragon roll wind'

6　恐龍 literally 'scary dragon'

7　反引力, 反重力 (詞彙：antigravity=anti+gravity; 參考 antibiotic, antibody)

8　龍膽紫 literally 'dragon gall purple'

9　保麗 / 力龍 also polystyrene; literally 'protecting beauty dragon' or 'protecting power dragon'

10　農家庭院 (詞彙 farmyard=farm+yard)

11　王警官 literally 'Wang Officer'

12　鈴木 Suziki (汽車品牌)

13　鳳凰 phoenix

Philosophy

哲

Chapter **08** / ⛈ Friday. Saturday. Sunday

Fear

By now I had to abandon the idea of Milkshake showing a preference for a new 'flavor' after just one week. If anything, he seemed to like Ting-Ting even more than before. The iceberg had not melted one little bit.

Oh, I was also wrong in assuming that Mr. Wu would let me get away with tiptoeing all over his vegetables and permanently stunting their growth. This particular Sunday morning, I looked out of my bedroom window and saw something that sent a chill down my spine. There he was —the farmer and Tai-Ji pretender—striding like a stern statesman over the beach to our humble little cabin. I was trapped. Nowhere to run. Nowhere to hide. Maybe Sunday mornings weren't always so peaceful after all...

He got nearer and nearer to the house. I couldn't move from the window. I watched him every step of the way. Mr. Wu was always frowning so I couldn't really tell if he was in a worse mood than usual, but he had armed himself with a flat basketball. I could see it in his chubby, soil-stained right hand. He looked very menacing indeed. And very determined.

The only pause in his firm stride came just meters from the house. You see, Mr. Wu's allergic to turtles, so he hesitated slightly when he saw Ro sunbathing outside the kitchen

Fear

window. To his credit, he soon regained his composure and made his way up the four steps to the front door. The knock was loud enough for even Ye-Ye to hear. But it wasn't loud enough to prevent me from staying frozen to my chair.

"Mr. Wu, what a nice surprise!" I heard Ye-Ye say as the door swung open. I knew there would be a big smile on Ye-Ye's wrinkled, guava-colored face. He's considered the most refined gentleman in the village—greets everyone with a big diplomatic smile, especially the most serious looking people. Nai-Nai always used to say that she fell in love with Ye-Ye because he had such charm and the good manners of a diplomat. She said he had an automatic smile, but he always made you feel that it was especially for you.

Mr. Wu was not a gentleman or a diplomat.
"Morning." he said roughly.
He rounded the cold greeting off with a formal nod of his well-tanned head. Then he just stood there, fiddling with his belt buckle and his basketball.
"And what can I do for you on this beautiful spring morning, Mr. Wu?" asked Ye-Ye, still smiling automatically.
Like an owl, Mr. Wu didn't seem to have any neck. He cleared his throat a little awkwardly as if he'd swallowed a needle or something.

"Um...Sorry to trouble you folks," he muttered.

Then he stood there for a while as if he couldn't remember why he was troubling us.

"Is that boy of yours around?" he asked eventually, pronouncing every word very slowly. "I want to give him this special basketball..."

"Why, Mr. Wu... That's extremely thoughtful of you. Thank you!" replied Ye-Ye, looking at the old, weathered basketball a little skeptically.

Mr. Wu had been gripping it firmly for the last minute or two and by now it was as flat as a large orange pancake.

"I believe he is here somewhere," continued my grandfather, "I think I just saw him come in after his surf."

Mr. Wu raised his eyebrows expectantly and pushed out his lips.

"Kobi," called Ye-Ye, answering his facial appeal. "Mr. Wu from down the road is here to see you."

I was frozen before but I felt very hot now all of a sudden. This was the last person in the world I wanted to see me. Was it the end? Would I be scarred for life—both mentally and physically? If Mr. Wu broke fifty or sixty bones in my body with a flat basketball and crippled me in my own house, in front of my only remaining family member, that would be terribly embarrassing. Okay, not as embarrassing

Fear

as Milkshake fainting and then declaring his love to Ting-Ting in front of half the school, but still...

The heat was running up every part of my body. It seemed to stop somewhere in my head because that's where I first broke out into a sweat. Maybe if I just sat there very quietly for a second, they'd think I was out somewhere. Or dead.
"Kobi, you haven't suddenly forgotten how to behave yourself, have you?" called Ye-Ye again patiently. "Come along, we don't want to be rude and keep our visitor waiting, now do we?"
"Come along, young man," echoed Mr. Wu. "I won't bite..."
Mr. Wu tried to smile too but only managed a reluctant raise of his top lip. This made him look a bit like a camel. If anyone could abuse a smile, it was Mr. Wu.

Okay. Time to face the music.[1] Courage, Kobi, courage! I'd never opened my bedroom door so slowly.
"Mr. Wu...he...hello" I said, suddenly developing a stutter and trying to hide the anxiety in my voice.
It pained me to say it but I added, "H...h...how nice to see you again."
"What took you so long, Kobi? I could have had a kidney transplant by now," joked the diplomat.
"Sorry, Ye-Ye—and Mr. Wu—sorry, I was just busy reading

the Confucian[2] *Analects*.[3] I couldn't put it down. I lose track of time and everything else when I read sometimes. All that philosophy stuff is great, isn't it?"

I know what you're thinking, but it was the first thing that came into my head, okay?

Of course, both Ye-Ye and Mr. Wu seemed a little surprised at this. But, luckily they didn't ask me exactly which philosophical words of wisdom had made me lose track of time and everything. Ye-Ye simply complimented me on my choice of reading material, and then showed us both to the kitchen table with a hospitable wave of his hand.

Mr. Wu and I both sat down as if each of our chairs had turned into a giant cactus.

Ye-Ye nevertheless looked pleased as punch.[4] He was like a carefree little girl arranging her dolls and presiding over a playtime tea party.

"Ah, is it not pleasant to study with constant perseverance and application? Is it not delightful to have friends visiting from far-off lands?"[5] quoted Ye-Ye.

Of course, I was far too terrified to notice the reference to what I was supposed to have just been reading. Luckily, Ye-Ye was far too busy enjoying his own cleverness to notice that I didn't notice.

"Can we offer you some tea, Brother Wu? I think we have some Oolong⁶ lying around here somewhere," said the little girl to her oldest doll.

"Uh...Uh..." Mr. Wu was still struggling to reproduce a clever quote of his own. Eventually he was forced to give up. Nothing clever came to mind.

Ye-Ye was a very sensitive man when it came to others' struggles, so he politely rescued our visitor after just one second of awkward silence.

"I was actually just on my way to the market to pick up some groceries and do some bargaining, Mr. Wu. I hope you don't mind," said Ye-Ye.

"Oh..." managed Mr. Wu.

"I always go bargain hunting on Sunday. It keeps me young!" said Ye-Ye with the energy of a man who didn't need to have any organs transplanted at all.

"Will the two of you be okay without me?"

Before Mr. Wu could reply, Ye-Ye turned to me. "Kobi, can you brew some tea, please? Should be some in that bottom left-hand cabinet."

Without me? Will you be okay without me? My heart, suddenly as heavy as an anchor, sank like any coward's would have. My final hour had arrived. Ye-Ye was going off 'hunting' to stay young and I was going to die young. All on my own!

My Sherlock brain interrupted me here. At least, it reminded me, there was one positive when it came to Ye-Ye leaving the two of us all alone. At least he wouldn't have to see me being tortured by a chubby little hermit, slash shadow boxer, slash gardener, under our own roof. Still, I was devastated. In my cowardly heart I was screaming, *Ye-Ye, Ye-Ye! Don't leave me!*

Mr. Wu, on the other hand, seemed to relax significantly at the prospect of it being just the two of us.

"No tea for me, thank you," he said, even though he seemed to nod in acceptance, "I've just had some soy milk. And," he added in a surprisingly charming manner, "we'll be completely fine on our own, Sir. Please, I really wouldn't want to interrupt your grocery shopping and bargain hunting."

Ye-Ye nodded politely and with one final charming smile turned towards the door.

"In that case, see you later, Kobi. You be nice to our guest now, you hear?"

My only ally and hope for survival—the only witness to the evil murder that was about to occur—closed the creaking door behind him. It was like I was on a sinking ship and the last lifeboat had sailed away without me. Mr. Wu and I were left staring at each other across the table. We were like

Fear

two amateur chess players sizing up the weakness in their opponent's eyes rather than in their strategies. Images of Mr. Wu disposing of my corpse beside some lonely creek or behind his tool shed were spinning through my head like a helicopter propeller. I watched him slowly place the flat basketball on the table as if it were a loaded rifle. His searching eyes were still on me. He was about to strike like a cobra!

But, he didn't strike. Instead, he just blinked once or twice and tried again to smile. The camel face reappeared. Then he leaned closer and said quietly, "I was going to break every stinking bone in your dirty, bony body, you little turtle-feeder, but...I want you to do something for me instead." Still fixing his eyes on me, he pulled a piece of scrap paper out of the left breast pocket of his fishing vest. On it, was an address. I recognized it—Mr. and Mrs. Wang's address.

註 解

1　片語：面對困難 Time to face the music.

2　Confucius (孔子) 的形容詞

3　論語 *Analects*

4　片語：樂不可支，春風得意。除了「拳打」之外，「punch」也有
　　潘趣酒（用酒和果汁做的飲料）的意思。

5　論語 1.1.：「學而時習之，不亦說乎？有朋自遠方來，不亦樂乎？」
　　These are the first two lines from *Analects*.

6　烏龍 literally 'dark dragon'

Paint

畫

Chapter **09** / Monday Morning

Another Favor

My heart almost stopped when Ting-Ting came up to me the next morning at school and said hi. I was sitting next to the osmanthus' bushes at the time. There I was, just innocently nibbling on those little airplane shaped cookies and minding my own business when, suddenly, the sweetest voice in the world addressed me as if in a dream.

"Hi Kobi."

After Milkshake's romantic announcement to the world last week, Ting-Ting had hardly said a word to anyone. Whispers, whistles, rumors and giggles followed her all around the school and through the town. She was very proud of her attendance record, so there was no way she would cut class, but I could tell that she didn't really want to be there. She hid away from everyone like a lone outsider. Of course, she avoided Milkshake himself as if he were toxic or some horrible tropical virus. She planned her routes from class to class with incredible accuracy and timing. So much so that they never even had to make eye contact once. This was probably a good thing because I think if their eyes had met—even accidentally—it might have resulted in Ting-Ting exploding like a firecracker and ceasing to exist. Naturally, I felt more sorry for her than I did for Milkshake and his big mouth, despite the fact that everyone made just as much fun of him. Even though she didn't say anything, her eyes told the whole painful story of what was going on in her mind. It gave me a stomachache to see Ting-Ting so sad.

"Hi Kobi," she said again, assuming that I hadn't heard her the first time.

"H...h...hello Ting-Ting." I nearly choked on a biscuit. Not cool.

"Kobi, I hate to be a bother, but...I need to ask you a favor."

My mind was racing like an ambulance. Okay, she wanted me to beat Milkshake up.[2] I looked down at my knuckles. They didn't look like they could beat anyone up. On second thought, maybe she was going to ask me to help her escape. She wanted to escape because she didn't want to put up with everyone teasing her all the time. Or maybe she... Don't worry, I didn't make a fool of myself and say something stupid like 'Ting-Ting, I would roll down Jade Mountain[3] in my underwear if you asked me.' Or 'Ting-Ting, I would sit on a barbecue for you', something like that. I didn't want her to think I had the IQ[4] of a pebble, now did I?

"Uh, sure thing, Ting-Ting. Of course. Uh...What is it?" I tried to make my reply as casual as possible. Secretly, I was holding my breath in anticipation.

"Well, I've got this art project that I have to finish for Miss Lin,[5] you see. It's a very important assignment."
Miss Lin's the art teacher by the way. She has long streaming hair like a dark and shiny silk scarf. Some say it's because her dad owns a barbershop. She's really pretty, even by Milkshake's standards. So why didn't my chest hurt when I saw Miss Lin?
"Uh...Whatever."

Whatever? What a stupid thing to say! Out of all the witty and charming things I could have said, I said 'whatever'. What an idiot. Pebble IQ. Loser. Definitely not cool. Auntie Guo's right, people who are in love—especially masculine people—are not very eloquent. Except for poets, they're special. Especially the really old ones. The ones who drown themselves in rivers. I'd never sound very poetic if I kept randomly using words like 'whatever'.
Ting-Ting looked slightly confused but continued nonetheless, "The only instructions she gave us were that we have to paint someone." She raised her eyebrows as if to make sure that I was listening. "Someone that we admire."
"Admire?"
Oh my God, Ting-Ting wanted me to model for her!
Oh my God, Ting-Ting admired me!

Of course, deep down I knew that it was probably too good
to be true. I was dreaming. But, my heart was singing with
joy for those brief seconds and I didn't want to interrupt
it. I didn't want to stop the music. Instead, I just pretended
that Ting-Ting had been longing to tell me that she admired
me for quite some time. I wanted so badly to believe that
it was only now, thanks to Miss Lin having assigned her
students such a task, that she finally had a way of telling me.
For those precious seconds, I was so filled with happiness,
that I thought I was going to burst and make an enormous
mess all over the osmanthus bushes. There was an 8.2 size
earthquake in my chest.

Ting-Ting must have noticed what was going on in my weird
little masculine mind because she suddenly smiled a bit shyly.
She'd seen the flicker of delight and expectation in my eyes.
I scratched the back of my head a little shyly too. Then, we
both burst out laughing. All the awkwardness had somehow
melted away. Oh, how I missed that perfect laughter!
"Maybe for my next project, Kobi," she smiled, once we
stopped laughing. "But this time I was...um...I was hoping I
could paint your turtle."

Laughter really is the best medicine. Even better than garlic. The old sparkle had returned to Ting-Ting's eyes already.

"Ro?"

"Please."

"You want to paint Ro-Ro Gway-Gway?"

"Yes, I admire him and I would like to paint him. First I'm going to sketch him, and then I'm going to paint his portrait."

I have to admit that I truly wasn't expecting to hear that. Lately, life was proving to be full of surprises.

"Uh...okay," I said, still a bit shocked. "I'll...I'll tell him after school."

Ting-Ting laughed again.

"Okay," she said winking a sparkly wink. "Tell him I'd like to schedule a meeting for Wednesday afternoon."

註解

1 桂花 literally 'osmanthus flower'
2 片語：痛打一頓 'to beat up'
3 玉山 Taiwan's highest mountain (3952m)
4 智商 Intelligence Quotient
5 林小姐 Lin is a common family name. Xiǎojie is common term of address for a young, unmarried woman

Wave

浪

Chapter **10** / 〰 Monday afternoon

Escape

First the seal, then Mr. Wu and now Ting-Ting. That's three visitors in a matter of only a couple of weeks. My head was swimming. It was swimming so much that I had no idea what Mr. Ma was talking about in Biology class that afternoon. From the very start of the lesson, I'd buried myself in my workbook, but secretly my mind was again wandering to all sorts of universes. Only once did I look up from my desk to see him pointing at the x-ray of a plant root system. Charts of plant root systems don't seem to help for swimming heads. I'm afraid they're not great at bringing you back from other universes either.

Of course, I don't remember anything else from the lesson. I simply had too much on my mind. One: I still felt sad about the seal. Two: I still had to work out how I was going to keep my promise to Mr. Wu. And three: the thought of an artistic angel like Ting-Ting casually dropping by and sketching my best friend in our little cabin, was simply driving me crazy. (Okay, to be honest, I'd never seen any of Ting-Ting's art before, but I was already her biggest fan.) In short, I was facing multiple thorny issues all piled up on top of one another. When it rains, it pours.[1]

Regarding Ting-Ting's visit, I know I should have been happy that the universe had finally decided to give me a helping hand and bring us together. But, instead, I just couldn't help feeling awfully anxious about Wednesday afternoon. It was like all my heart muscles were tangled up in a little ball. My head was like a deep gorge full of endless echoes. Like when you stand up too quickly and feel very dizzy. I was never more dizzy. There was only one way to clear my mind. To silence all the voices in my head. It wasn't Watermelon, Watermelon, Tai-Ji Land, Far Away.[2] It was the ocean.

When I got home from school, I was really pleased to see Ro sitting at the top of his slide waiting for me with almost human impatience. I changed as quickly as I could and grabbed my board. I didn't bother with wax, I just wanted to get in amongst the waves as soon as possible. The salty water would wash everything away. And if it didn't wash everything away, at least it would cover it all up for a while so I could breathe.

"There was only one way to clear my mind. It wasn't Watermelon, Watermelon, Tai-Ji Land, Far Away."

"It always reminded me of that picture of the
elephant that had been swallowed by a snake."

I rushed down to the beach. For once, Ro and I reached
the water simultaneously. It was freezing, but the sun was
shining and the seawater[3] smelled fresh and alive. I took
in deep breaths as I paddled out to where the waves were
breaking. Far off in the distance, a couple of fishing boats
and local tourist ferries were slowly but surely gliding
across the sea. Turtle Island lay in the background, still and
magnificent on the horizon. It always reminded me of that
picture of the elephant that had been swallowed by a snake.
You know—the one drawn by that French alien in the fancy
suit.[4]

It wasn't summer yet, and weekdays, especially Mondays, are
great. There were hardly any other surfers around. Today,
we were extra lucky because, apart from one or two hang-

gliders[5] high up in the clouds, it was just the two of us. We didn't mind sharing the waves with other folks, but when your head is swimming and you can't breathe properly, I think it's permissible to be a little bit selfish. Ro's long neck was sticking out of the water about thirty meters from the shore. He was waiting for me. I laughed and paddled a little faster.

Before I could reach him, a large smooth bulge appeared on the dark surface of the water. Ro had seen the large wave approaching and started swimming back towards the beach. He was moving rapidly, but his head remained perfectly still above the surface. I couldn't have had a better view as the rising face of the wave picked him up and lifted him into the air. For a few split seconds, it seemed like Ro was suspended at the top of the wave. He was surrounded by white foam and spray. Then, at just the right moment and with powerful precision, his flippers emerged out of the steep blue-green curtain with just one or two playful strokes.

Then, there was a quick burst of energy. In a flash, he had elegantly flipped onto his back just as the wave was starting to curl like a sleepy flower petal. Riding on his leathery back, a picture of perfect balance, the cinnamon-loving turtle started skimming down the smooth surface of the wave at great speed. His carapace[6] carved into the water.

It cut seven crisp white lines (all leatherback turtles have seven ridges on their backs) all along the curling petal to the bottom of the wave. Only Ting-Ting's back is more beautiful.

Although tiny compared to the wave, Ro was in complete control. The wall of water came crashing down with tremendous speed and power, but he looked like he had all the time in the world. He even had time for one or two counterclockwise rotations. Then he subtly tilted his body at an angle and shot quickly to the right, vanishing into a blue green tunnel of water. He was now inside what surfers call the 'green room'. It's a place where time stops and thinking disappears.

"...a picture of perfect balance."

Now, I don't know if turtles are capable of such a thing, but I somehow knew Ro was smiling from ear to ear.[7] I realized that I'd stopped thinking about everything else too.

註解

1　片語：禍不單行 'when it rains it pours'
2　還記得吳先生在第五章很優雅的固定太極拳動作嗎？ Remember Mr. Wu's elegant Tai Ji routine in Chapter 5?
3　海水 (詞彙 seawater=sea+water)
4　《小王子》 The Little Prince, by Antoine de Saint-Exupér 裡面提到的一張圖片，對大人來說是一頂帽子，只有小朋友看得出來其實是一條吞了大象的蟒蛇。
5　滑翔運動者 (詞彙 hang, glide)
6　甲殼 type of turtle shell
7　棱皮龜和其他烏龜及鳥一樣只有內耳，沒有外耳 Like birds, leatherbacks and other turtles have no outer ears. They have inner ears only.

Dance

舞

Chapter **11** / Tuesday

Milkshake Takes the Bait[1]

On Tuesday I decided that Milkshake and I couldn't avoid each other forever. I decided that we were both being stubborn and silly. The last time he hadn't spoken to me for an entire week was when we were six years old. On that occasion, I had broken his Rubik's Cube[2] beyond repair with a rubber hammer. Anyway, I knew we couldn't go on like this. The stubbornness was bound to start suffocating us sooner or later. Besides, it wasn't very mature, was it? I had to try to be a little bit more open-minded[3] about the whole thing and break through the barrier of silence between us. That's another advantage of having a surfing turtle for a best friend, by the way. It makes you try to be more objective.

He suspected that I liked Ting-Ting, and I knew that he loved her. Still, we couldn't let this minor complication ruin a perfectly good friendship. The only way to solve matters was for the two of us to go fishing out by Black Stone Harbor.[4] As far as I knew, that was by far the best way to have a good heart-to-heart without actually saying anything. This approach normally works with guys. Fishing and not saying anything can bridge just about any gulf that might exist between male friends. Well, not always, but it was worth a try.

On Tuesdays, Milkshake doesn't have to help out at the teahouse. So, as all of us were leaving Chinese class that morning, I decided to take my chances.

"Hey, Shakes...wait up!" I called through the stream of students rushing out the door.

Milkshake turned around slowly.

He was obviously trying to hide the surprise in his voice when he replied, "Kobi...What's up?"

He was still busy packing an ancient Chinese poetry textbook into his One Piece[5] schoolbag.

"Not much, Shakes, not much." I said, putting on a friendly face. "Hey, are you doing anything this afternoon?"

Milkshake's eyes strayed to one side. He was a realistic guy, so he wasn't sure if I was inviting him somewhere or if I was scheduling a time for a fight.

"I was going to...uh...going to wash the dog. Mom's been nagging me for ages."

"Go fishing with me first. I'll help you shampoo Oscar when we get back. I'll bring the bait."

There were one or two fishermen already sitting at the dock chatting and joking when we arrived. They were toothless and gray but they laughed like naughty little schoolboys on a camping trip. Like little boy scouts who'd just found a bra in the woods. The light drizzle that had started to fall didn't bother them at all and they looked happier than a pair of ants in a soda can.

Milkshake Takes the Bait

"That's us a few decades from now, Kobi!" joked Milkshake as we took a stroll along the pier towards them.

He was in a much better mood now that he was sure there wasn't going to be a fight. Not today anyway.

"Yep," I answered with a smile, "and a few decades from now you'll still be catching all the fish."

Milkshake laughed silently and tugged on his wrinkled Batman[6] T-shirt with one hand, thumbing his nose at the sky with the other. He liked to be reminded of the fact that he was a far superior fisherman.

"Don't worry, Kobi," he said, "you'll still be catching all the waves."

We passed by one or two fishing boats that were busy docking in the harbor. Eventually, we found a suitable spot near the water's edge. We folded out our chairs. Milkshake opened a small case filled with all kinds of fishing gear.

We carefully baited our hooks and spent a few moments surveying the water. The sea was very still today, like a massive lake. The docks seemed to be floating on a giant fishbowl.[7] A clear blue sky and one or two clouds were mirrored in the surface of the water. It was so calm that we could even see a few blurry, scaly shapes darting this way and that beneath the surface.

Having cast our lines into the water, we settled into our folding chairs. We rested our rods on our knees. The old men were still chattering away cheerfully to our right. A couple of seagulls were hovering overhead, investigating the four of us. One of the fishermen had brought a little radio and some classic Taiwanese songs were playing in the background. Milkshake and I whiled away the time, talking and gossiping on the pier. We were talking far more than I expected.

The greatest excitement of the afternoon was provided by a seagull exactly one hour later. This fearless bird ventured much closer to the old men's bait boxes than it should have. Despite clapping their hands and shooing and shouting, the seagull remained only slightly intimidated and kept advancing. Finally, one of the men jumped up impatiently on skinny wrinkled legs, and started waving his arms around in the air. He looked like a mad conductor attempting to finish a symphony in double time.[8] Mr. Xu[9] once told me that an ape's arms are longer than its legs. Cool. We'll get back to Mr. Xu later; there's no time now.

When waving his arms around didn't succeed in scaring the bird away, the old fisherman grabbed his fishing rod. Violently, he thrust it this way and that in a most threatening manner. This however, did not seem to frighten the gull at all. The poor old chap kept thrusting blindly. Unfortunately, the final thrust was so powerful that his old knees instantly buckled underneath him. This sent him into a clumsy clockwise ballet spin that knocked over both boxes—as well as his own fishing buddy—in a miniature hurricane of old bones and recreational equipment. The seagull, completely unharmed, crowed triumphantly from a safe height.

With the rod warrior trying to help his friend up, the two old souls were soon in a terrible tangle. Milkshake and I couldn't help it, we were laughing uncontrollably. We must have laughed a little more hysterically than was socially acceptable. I know this because when we looked up again, the seagull had been completely forgotten and the two fishing rods were waving towards us! If they couldn't take revenge on the awful bird, they were determined to take it on someone else! Of course, we weren't deliberately trying to taunt the old gentlemen but there was no time for apologies or pleading innocence! Grabbing our things and not daring to look back, we surrendered without a moment's hesitation and fled[10] down the road as fast as our young legs could carry us. We certainly didn't want any additional entertainment at our own expense, that's for sure. Not carrying a single catch, but not having been caught either, we giggled all the way home.

Safely back at Milkshake's house, we took some sponges and buckets outside. We were going to wash Oscar the dog under the tap in the yard. Of course, Oscar was quite humiliated by being washed under a tap in full view of all the neighbors' dogs. That's why we had to bribe him with an outrageous amount of dog biscuits and back rubs, otherwise he would never have agreed. Thanks to all the treats and caresses he received in the process, he endured the washing with great dignity.

"You're spoiling that dog, man. Can dogs get diabetes?" I asked as Milkshake reached into the bag of biscuits for the sixth bribe of the afternoon. "If not, he's still going to develop some kind of eating disorder with all these treats flying around."
Milkshake paused for a second and raised his left eyebrow playfully.
"It's the only way to prevent him from running away, Kobi. No biscuits, no obedience. You know that. Even when we play fetch, I need to take along a bag of baby carrot sticks. Otherwise he'll start growling—even pee on my boots—if I throw something!"

"You can't be serious," I cut in.

"Of course I'm serious, it's the only thing that works. I
know it's wrong in a way but who cares? Besides, you're not
exactly stingy with the cinnamon either, Kobi. I've seen how
you give Ro-Ro Gway-Gway some whenever he wants. He
doesn't even have to beg or fetch or be washed like Oscar.
Not to mention the skateboard slide and the swimming pool
you built for him. If he's not soaking, surfing or satisfying
his turtle hunger, he's baking in the sun like a—sorry to
make a comparison with such an inferior animal but—like a
lizard. He's practically staying in a five star reptile hotel!
No wonder he keeps coming back!"

I couldn't argue with any of that, so I didn't even try.
Besides, I was quite proud of the fact that one of the
largest sea turtles in the world kept coming back. And that
he could indulge in all kinds of luxuries right there in our
backyard! And that he was my friend.

"Friends come first, right?" I laughed. "FCF!"

Oscar gave a bark of approval.

"Yep," smiled Milkshake, "FCF!"

By now, our furry friend was completely covered in soapy
white foam. The time had come to bring up the subject of
Ting-Ting. Of course, I had to do so with great tact. If I

wasn't careful, I'd embarrass Milkshake, or make him angry, or maybe both. Then, all the time we'd spent fishing—without actually catching anything—would have been an awful waste. When I was sure that Oscar's paws and the dark curls of fur behind his ears were as clean as a whistle, I stopped scrubbing, cleared my throat and looked up.

"I think Oscar needs a girlfriend, dude" I said.
Oscar's floppy ears were suddenly completely erect. He could scent something meaningful in the air.
"Girlfriend?"
"Yep. Biscuits are fine and all, but I doubt whether it's really enough. Dogs are like their masters. What he needs... is some companionship. Maybe even a touch of romance."
"Companionship? Romance?" Milkshake's face had screwed up like a bitter melon."

"Yeah, you know, friends and five star things are great but what he really requires is a female companion."
"Female?" Milkshake's voice seemed to be going higher and higher.
I smiled and said slightly mockingly, "You do know what a female is, don't you?"
If Milkshake suspected where this conversation was going,

or what I was actually implying, his face didn't show it.
Instead, he smiled back at me and replied, "Sure, it's the
thing that you're the most afraid of in this world, right?"

When we finally both stopped pretending to laugh,
Milkshake turned the faucet back on and picked up the hose.
He started rinsing the foam off his dog's back and shoulders.
Slowly but surely, the soapy white bundle turned back into
obedient, well-fed Oscar. I made up my mind that it was now
or never.
"Shakes...I was thinking...I was thinking maybe I would try
and get one as well."
"What? A dog?" he asked. "Whatever you do, don't get a
furry one, Kobi. Look, they take ages to wash. No, no, trust
me. Turtles are much better. You just..."
"Uh...No," I interrupted him, "I was thinking I should also get
a...a companion."

The word sounded so strange when I said it this time.
Companion. Like it was something you could order in the
mail, or catch at the clinic if you're weren't careful.
Both eyebrows went up on this occasion as Milkshake
nearly sprayed water all over the floor.
"You mean a girlfriend?"

"Uh-huh" I nodded. "Hey, do we have to dry Oscar as well?"
I asked, trying to soften the blow.

A full two minutes went by as Milkshake thoroughly washed
the remaining soap bubbles off the soaked animal. (I must
remember to tell you another soap bubble story later on!)

"Have anyone in mind?" He asked at last, trying to sound
indifferent. He completely ignored the issue of dog drying
for the moment.

"Uh...I dunno...maybe the girl from the fruit shop. What do
you think?"

註 解

1 片語：除了帶魚餌之外，也有 '上鉤' 的意思 *'to take the bait'*
2 魔術方塊 literally *'magic block'*
3 心胸寬大，能接受新思想；無先入之見，無偏見的
4 烏石港 literally 'dark stone harbor'; small harbor town situated on the east coast of Taiwan in Yilan County
5 海賊王 popular Japanese manga and anime
6 蝙蝠俠 (詞彙 Batman=bat+man)
7 魚缸 (詞彙 fishbowl=fish+bowl)
8 快步行進 (NOT 'taking twice as long')
9 徐先生 literally Xú Mister; Xu is a common family name
10 flee 過去式 fled
11 苦瓜 bitter melon

Beach

灘

Chapter **12** / Tuesday Evening

Stories

I'm always amazed at how many stories wash up on the beach. Old shirt buttons, instant noodle wrappers, toy cars with missing wheels, dead crabs; they all have their stories. They've all come from somewhere. They've all been somewhere. They've all done stuff. I like thinking about their stories because then I don't have to think about mine. People waste so much time thinking about their own stories.

Music

樂

Chapter 13 / Wednesday Morning

Tongues, Luck & Yellow Umbrellas

When I woke up the next morning, it felt like I'd barely slept. I'd had a very vivid dream that there were lots of clothes pins pinching my tongue and that my arms were too short to reach them. I tried to tell everyone what was wrong but no one could understand me. Scary. I was obviously still really nervous about the 'girl from the fruit shop' coming over that afternoon, worried that I wouldn't know what to say to her. This was an emergency.

There was only one way I could prepare myself. I had to go to the library and speak to Auntie Guo. She was a very peculiar individual (some would say crazy) but she was the only person who could calm me down in a situation like this. Besides, out of everyone I knew, I probably valued her opinion the most. So, after hugging Ye-Ye quickly and giving Ro a few light taps on his left flipper, I grabbed a couple of warm steamed buns[1] and rushed out the door. I almost forgot to put on my school shoes.

I wasn't going to risk cutting through Mr. Wu's garden again. Well, at least not until I had accomplished the mission he had given me. For now, his property was strictly out of bounds, no matter how late I was. Running hard, I took the long way around to the library. Along the way, I overtook Mr. Xu who was on his way to the bakery to pick up his breakfast. Mr.

Tongues, Luck & Yellow Umbrellas

Xu runs the local hardware store and his breakfast always consists of the same thing: a pork floss pancake[2] and a cup of Job's Tears milk.[3]

"Morning, Mr. Xu!" I said as I sped past him at a pedestrian crossing.

Okay, both of us were actually jaywalking but that's not important. (What's important is that you don't tell Officer Wang!) I was going so fast that I nearly disturbed his wig. Luckily I didn't because Mr. Xu is quite famous for his vanity. His fancy French wig is always combed from right to left in a huge, perfectly uniform wave. Ro could spin around at least six or seven times on that wave. The tip of it usually just touches his left eyebrow. The latter is permanently raised like that of a person who suspects someone else has been using their toothbrush.[4]

I'd given him a bit of a fright, so a short "hello" was all he could manage as he swung round clutching his head. Seeing that it was me, he smiled briefly and then commenced a frantic search for his reflection in the nearest scooter mirror. The wig wave was out of place. I think people care more about fake hair than real hair.

"Hey, Mr. Xu, a crocodile is the only animal that can't stick out its tongue! See you!" I yelled.

We like to trade animal facts now and then to test each other's biological knowledge. We're quite competitive. Because of Mr. Xu, I definitely read more biology books than most people my age. And because of me, Mr. Xu watches more *Animal Planet*[5] than he should.

By the time the distant reply about toads being able to breathe through their skin followed a few seconds later, I was already too far away to hear it.

Auntie Guo was busy unlocking the main doors when I reached the library gate. She was dressed in a fashionable pink blouse and a black skirt. A light pink silk scarf was draped around her slender neck. Her Coke-colored hair was done up like an elegant anchorwoman's. I could hardly speak. I was excited and out of breath.

"Auntie Guo!" I called as I approached the building at a gallop.

"Is that you, Kobi?" she said looking up in surprise. "What brings you here so early in the morning, my boy?"

I ran all the way up to the door, nearly knocking her over.

"Auntie Guo! I have to consult you on something really important!"

"Calm down, child, you'll have a fit!" she said calmly. "If people find you here having died of excitement in my doorway I'll have to take the blame, you know. Catch your breath first, or I won't let you in," she smiled.

I threw down my schoolbag and placed my palms on my knees, breathing heavily. Auntie Guo was patting me gently on the back.

"That's better. Now, make a proper effort to stop sweating and then you can come inside and tell me whatever it is that's so important. I think that's reasonable. I'll turn on the kettle in the meantime..."

A short while after the pink blouse had disappeared into the building, I picked up my bag and followed it inside. The familiar smell of old books greeted me as I entered. I felt calmer already.

"Would you like some tea, my dear? The water's just come to a boil."

"No thanks, Auntie Guo."

"How about some fresh rice milk?[6] We can share—as long as you don't tell anyone that I like to mix it with my coffee."

(What on earth would Milkshake say about a beverage like that?!)

She winked at me and brought a finger to her lips to indicate that the bizarre combination was to remain a secret.

I smiled to show that I would keep the revelation completely confidential and this pleased her.

"Oh, or would you prefer some orange juice?" she continued.

"I have some of that too... here somewhere."

I just shrugged my shoulders. Too many choices can sometimes make it hard to choose.

"C'mon child, don't just stand there like a mummy!" she said. "Follow me, we can have our breakfast together."

At the back of the library was a small kitchen. Actually, it was a kitchen, a study and an office all rolled into one. It had one or two household appliances, a tiny wooden table, three chairs, a small DVD[7] collection and an old CD[8] player. That's all Auntie Guo needed because she was quite a lousy cook to be honest. Even instant noodles posed a challenge. On one of the chairs sat a broken typewriter. Auntie Guo used to be an editor for the local newspaper, by the way. She said she quit because her exclusive editorials were largely wasted on the local population. She said local populations never appreciate anything. She also used to be a music teacher, so she always tunes into her favorite classical music radio broadcast over breakfast. Soon the air was filled with piano notes and the fragrant scent of rice milk, coffee, steamed buns, fried radish cake[9] and soy sauce. She always says life is like a drawing; if you want to color it in, you need good music.

"Bon appetite,[10] Kobi! You know the golden rule, right?"

"You know the golden rule, right?"

she reminded me as she swayed her head to Debussy's "Arbaesque No.1."[11]

Auntie Guo's golden rule is that you have to close your eyes while you're eating. She says if your eyes are busy, your mind and your tongue both get lazy. That's because visual input, she says, is too powerful a distraction. She believes that if you open your eyes, you empty your brain. Anyway, I didn't mind abiding by this rule, somehow the food normally tasted better that way. It's very pleasant. Plus, closing my eyes while eating always allowed me to think of some abstract and profound ideas. You know, things you wouldn't normally think of if you had your eyes open. Like how would an elephant eat spaghetti. Or who was the first person on Earth to say 'surf the Internet.'

Today I found myself pondering the amazing set of coincidences I wanted to tell you about earlier. About how, around two years ago, the forces of the universe somehow conspired to ensure that Brother Liao saved Ye-Ye's life. I mean, how he saved Ye-Ye's life in his sleep while riding someone else's scooter—riding someone else's scooter naked down the wrong alley.

It all happened one rainy afternoon. Ye-Ye was walking down a narrow alley on the way to play Dark Chess[12] with his old mate, Ah-Dai.[13] It being rainy and all, Ye-Ye had his head buried under a large soybean yellow umbrella. Noticing that one of his shoelaces was loose, Ye-Ye knelt down on the right side of the alley to tie it.

Now, you wouldn't think lacing up a shoe could involve such grave danger, but...all of a sudden, one of those little blue trucks...you know the ones that drive faster than a landslide and are forever honking at everybody else? Anyway, one of those little blue trucks came rocketing around the bend. Unfortunately, raindrops were drumming loudly on his umbrella and poor Ye-Ye didn't hear the peril approaching. The driver of the little blue truck rocket wasn't aware of Ye-Ye either. He was too busy opening a little bottle of Savage Bull.[14] Besides, he was going too fast anyway. Even if he had spotted Ye-Ye, there was no way he could've braked in time.

By the time he came around the corner in his little blue bullet and the blurred image of a bright yellow umbrella appeared in his rainy windshield, it was too late. In an instant, he was struck by the realization that he was about to run over a bright yellow umbrella. And its very short owner of course. (Ye-Ye was still kneeling down at the time, so the umbrella was very low to the ground.) The driver barely had a second to slam on the brakes, close his eyes and say a quick prayer to the half-starved, red-faced god of protection.

At that precise moment, the hero of this humorous anecdote, Brother Liao, entered the scene. Having had too many bottles of beer for lunch, he came speeding around the bend from the opposite direction, enjoying his afternoon nap, naked and on a scooter of which he was not the owner. Now, the Seven Lucky Gods[15] must really like Ye-Ye because what took place that day in that fateful alley is totally unbelievable. I'll explain why. You see, that afternoon, a drunk Brother Liao had gotten out of bed without waking up, grabbed his favorite pillow and staggered out of the house.

"...the Seven Lucky Gods must really like Ye-Ye" (extract below)

Still asleep and still hugging the pillow under one arm, he had stumbled down the road like a lame duck. Somehow he had hopped on the nearest scooter. The latter happened to belong to Mr. Wu, who unfortunately had left his keys in his bike on this occasion. Brother Liao, stripped down to only his birthday suit,[16] mounted the vehicle. Then, eyes firmly shut, he set off in the direction of a 'wrong alley'.

As he did so, he picked up speed. When he reached the sharp bend where Ye-Ye was tying his shoelace, he also was going too fast. The tread on Mr. Wu's scooter tires were quite worn out from chasing trespassers and stray dogs. So, naturally, they slid like a bar of soap on the wet

Tongues, Luck & Yellow Umbrellas

surface of the road. The scooter had turned into a sled. Now horizontal, it went scraping along the tar like a cola bottle. Brother Liao, on the other hand, had taken off into the rainy sky. Propelled by his beer belly's considerable momentum, he was flying through the air like an astronaut. Some say what occurred next was just a freak occurrence, but to me it was an absolute miracle. Fast asleep[17] but instinctively clinging to his pillow, the flying Brother Liao collided with the unsuspecting Ye-Ye, knocking him off the road and out of the way of the little blue missile.

When the little blue missile pilot opened his eyes, there was Savage Bull all over his lap. His truck was on top of Mr. Wu's scooter and Brother Liao was on top of Ye-Ye with a bright yellow umbrella and a Hello Kitty pillow in-between the two survivors. Now, imagine what a hit that would have been on Youtube!

Remarkably, the only damage was the jagged[18] scrapes all along the sides of Mr. Wu's scooter as well as the bottom of the truck. The pillow hadn't lost a feather and even the umbrella was largely intact. However, the most miraculous of all was that neither Ye-Ye, nor Brother Liao, was seriously injured. In fact, they hardly had any injuries at all!

They should have both split their skulls open. Somehow, the pillow had cushioned Brother Liao's fall and absorbed virtually the whole impact of the collision. Hello Kitty had prevented a most unfortunate disaster. Ye-Ye—apart from a sprained ankle and a large rip in his trousers—didn't have a scratch! Brother Liao's crooked nose was bleeding a little and his bottom jaw got bruised a bit. The bloody nose had resulted from the tip of the yellow umbrella accidentally entering the drowsy alcoholic's left nostril when he touched down. The bruise on the jaw was from when he finally woke up and hit himself to see if he was dreaming. The driver of the little blue truck wasn't harmed at all, but his pants were Savage Bull sticky.

I heard the sound of chopsticks, knives, forks and empty plates and containers being removed from the table. I slowly raised my eyelids and looked down. My pleasant breakfast had somehow disappeared in a cloud of smoke. My stomach was surprisingly full.

"Kobi, that was absolutely delightful. I was just thinking about spaghetti and elephants. Very relaxing."

"Really? I was just..."

"But, I'm afraid you'll have to tell me what's on your mind next time." Auntie Guo winked sweetly, cutting me off in the middle of my sentence.

Tongues, Luck & Yellow Umbrellas

"But Auntie Guo..." I protested.

The protest, however, fell on deaf ears.
"We'll have to further our discussion at some point in the future, my dear boy. Otherwise you'll be late for school! Don't worry, it'll give you more time to think it over."
"But..."
"I'll accompany you on a journey into the depths of your soul next time, Kobi, but for now we'll have to skip it. C'mon..."
"But..."
"No buts, dear boy, I'll make it up to you next time. You need to go to school and I need to dye my hair. Then I have to meditate. After that, I have to go for a long jog and renew my membership at the golf club. Those are things no woman could possibly postpone."
"Buuuttt..."
"I don't care how persistent you are, Kobi, or how long your 'buts' are. It's time to go! You heard me, march! No time like the present![19] Besides, you know I never give in. I can't afford to with my schedule."

Of course, I was well aware that there was no way I'd win an argument with the highly articulate Auntie Guo, but arguers my age are always hopeful.

My shoes felt like lead as I reluctantly made my way to the door.

"Oh, one last thing," said Auntie Guo.

"Yes?" I turned around hopefully.

"I need you to convey an urgent message to Miss Lin for me."

"Oh." I said, very disappointed.

Auntie Guo ignored the disappointment completely. "Please tell her to get in touch with me, would you? The latest edition of *Nail Nourishment Weekly* has just come in."

I raised an eyebrow. "Urgent?"

"Don't look at me like that, Kobi. If you knew how informative those magazines were, you'd understand. And if you saw Miss Lin's nails, you'd understand the true meaning of urgency.

I made one last feeble attempt to object and somehow prolong the consultation, but by this time the librarian had already skillfully escorted me to the door. I stood helpless as she promptly closed it behind me.

註 解

1 饅頭

2 肉鬆蛋餅 literally 'meat loose egg cake'; fried egg pancake filled with sweet dried pork shavings

3 薏仁漿 milk made from the Job's Tears barley

4 牙刷 (詞彙 toothbrush=tooth+brush)

5 動物星球電視頻道

6 米漿

7 詞彙 Digital Versatile Disk (Disc)

8 詞彙 Compact Disk (Disc)

9 蘿蔔糕 also turnip cake, white radish cake

10 吃飯之前常用的法文片語 , 意思為 : (望你) 胃口大好，請慢用。'bon' 有 '好' 的意思，'appetit' 有胃口的意思 (詞彙 bonus, appetite)

11 法國古典音樂家德布西的《阿拉貝斯克第一號》

12 暗棋 board game; variation of Chinese Chess

13 阿呆

14 蠻牛 literally 'savage bull'; popular Taiwanese energy drink

15 七福神 literally 'seven blessing gods'; gods in Japanese mythology said to bring good fortune and prosperity

16 片語：跟出生的那時刻一樣赤條條的 *'in one's birthday suit'* (詞彙 birthday, suit)

17 睡得很熟 *'to be fast asleep'*

18 『形容詞 』鋸齒狀 ; 凹凸不平的

19 現在是做某事的最佳時機 , 不要再拖 , 不要再延擱 *'There's no time like the present.'* (詞彙 present tense)

Sour

酸

Chapter **14** / Wednesday Afternoon

Plans and Apologies

Wednesday afternoon had finally arrived. I wasn't ready for it. My visit to the library that morning hadn't done me any good at all. Despite her wonderful hospitality, I hadn't had an opportunity to disclose my secret to Auntie Guo. It was eating me up. On top of that, I knew for a fact that Milkshake was still in love with Ting-Ting. How did I know? Well, because he threw a wet sponge at me yesterday when I innocently mentioned 'the girl from the fruit store.' The bucket of water followed soon after, but by then, I'd already jumped the hedge like a horse and was halfway down the road. Basically, I couldn't seem to solve any of my problems lately.

You can imagine the mental state I was in. Ting-Ting would be here any minute. A million thoughts were galloping through my head like a herd of wild buffalo. One of them was about clothespins pinching my tongue. Isn't it funny how, when you like someone that much you actually dread seeing them? Okay, maybe that's a bit of an exaggeration, but I really had never been this anxious before. On top of everything else, I still had to figure out how I was going to fulfill Mr. Wu's odd request in exchange for him not breaking all of my bones. Since that angel from the fruit shop isn't here yet, it's probably a good idea to finally reveal what that particular request was. After all, it has been a while since I first mentioned it, and I need something to take my mind off how nervous I am.

It was all quite simple really. Mr. Wu wanted me to help him get revenge. Revenge a. on Brother Liao for ruining his scooter, and b. on Officer Wang for always boasting about all the fines he's given him.

"Two bad birds with one stone, Kobi," Mr. Wu had said on Sunday when he paid me a visit. "Two bad birds."

Okay, so it wasn't that simple. Responsibilities, friendships, blood ties, and the fact that Officer Wang was a policeman all severely complicated the matter. Now, I have to admit that, on the one hand, I felt obliged to compensate Mr. Wu. For one thing, I was often trespassing on his property. This wasn't good for his vegetable garden or for his blood

"Two bad birds."

pressure. Secondly, was it not Mr. Wu's scooter that had, in a way, saved Ye-Ye's life in that rainy alley that day? If it hadn't been for his misfortune of having a naked man steal his motorbike, and for the worn out tires on that vehicle, Ye-Ye might not be with us today. I was Ye-Ye's grandson. I owed him.

However, on the other hand, I was also deeply indebted to Brother Liao. Was it not the drunk, sleeping, naked Brother Liao who had also saved my only grandfather's life in that rainy alley?! Why, if he hadn't been flying through the air with his pillow at that exact moment, Ye-Ye would have been toast! In his own unique way, Brother Liao was a hero. On top of that, he'd helped me with my banana surfboard. How could I forget that?!

Mr. Wu or Brother Liao? Brother Liao or Mr. Wu? As you can see, it presented a significant moral dilemma. Either way, I knew I'd feel guilty whether I assisted Mr. Wu in carrying out his elaborate plan or not. It didn't make the decision any easier. While I'm wrestling with the impossible choice, we might as well look at the scheme in a little more detail. The plan relied on two key factors. The first was to get Brother Liao drunk. The second was to park Officer

Wang's scooter outside Brother Liao's house. If all went according to plan, and with a bit of luck, Officer Wang's scooter would end up somewhere parked on a red line under a small blue truck.

Mr. Wu was to execute the first step of the plan. He would lose some random bet with Brother Liao and then treat him to a few cans of beer outside the local High Life[1] convenience store. This would be much cheaper than a pub, especially if he spiked the beers with something stronger. His partner in crime, Kobi, would then have to take care of Step 2. Even though I wanted to cooperate with my neighbor, I have to confess something. The thought of stealing a police officer's scooter (a police officer who was also married to my school principal) sent icy, icy shivers down my spine. However, it was probably the only way I could prevent Mr. Wu from ripping it (my spine) out.

There was a knock on the door. My heart was pounding up and down like a drum in my breast. She was here. I tried to come up with the coolest possible thing I could say to Ting-Ting as I opened the door, but all of I could think of was... "I'm opening the door now..."

On the one hand I was a little disappointed to see that it

wasn't Ting-Ting who was standing outside our door. On the other, I was secretly quite relieved she hadn't been the one who had to hear me say something so uncool.

"Milkshake? Hi...hi dude. Uh...what are you doing here?"
I glanced a little anxiously behind him just to make sure that Ting-Ting wasn't close by. Or any buckets and sponges for that matter. Milkshake usually didn't believe in violence, but after yesterday, I wasn't so sure anymore. If he knew Ting-Ting was coming over to my house, he was sure to be hurling some weapon much harder than a sponge at me. Something like a sneaker or maybe even a guava. Ouch.

Milkshake looked a little ashamed and was adjusting his glasses uncomfortably with his left hand. With his right, he was poking himself gently in the waist with a twig.
"Kobi..." he finally said. "I...uh...um...Look, I'm not good at this sort of thing."
"Okay?"
"But, look, I wanted to...uh...what's the word? I wanted to apologize for yesterday."
"Oh. Milkshake. Really?"
"Yeah man, look, I...I didn't mean to chase you away. Or..."
"Shakes, really. Don't worry about it, please."

"And I didn't mean to throw stuff at you. Hard stuff. You know I don't really believe in violence."

"I wasn't hurt at all, Milkshake. Really. Honestly, let's just forget it ever happened."

I hoped my impatience wasn't too obvious. Of course, I appreciated the apology, but all I could think of was that I had to speed it up. Ting-Ting would be here any minute!

"Let's put it all behind us, Milkshake. What's done, is done. Water under the bridge.² Honestly, no hard feelings." I smiled adding, "Besides, you throw like an old man."

Milkshake smiled as well. "Really? Still friends? That's very cool of you, Kobi. Very cool indeed. Thanks. Thanks a lot!"

We'd made peace. We were friends again. Now I just had to get rid of him. Unfortunately, Milkshake had no intention of leaving just yet. After hesitating for a short while he continued, half covering his mouth with a tea stained hand.

"Uh...Kobi?"

"Uh-huh?"

I could tell by the tone of his voice that something peculiar was about to come out of his mouth.

"Uh...Kobi, my man, I also wanted to ask you if you could... um...If you could...um...If you could give me a chance first."

"A chance?" I felt a strange sensation in the pit of my
stomach.

Milkshake was swaying to and fro like he had vicious bugs
in his pants or something. The twig battering his hip had
started poking a little harder. I thought it was going to come
out the other side.

"Yeah," he went on slowly, "I was hoping you could give me a
chance to ask her out first. You know, face to face. I...I just
want to make sure whether she likes me or not."

"Ask her first?" What was I hearing?!

Now it was my turn to look a bit uncomfortable. I think I
looked like someone who had just bitten into a grapefruit
when in fact they were expecting a tangerine. A sour
sensation had taken over my mouth.

"Yeah, you know, before you tell her that you like her."

"Oh...Shakes...Wow."

I suddenly had visions of a Great Wall of China[3] being
erected between myself and Ting-Ting. And I didn't think I
could stomach it.

"Wow." I said again. The sourness was everywhere.

The two of us stood there in awkward silence for at least
half a minute. It wasn't easy, but I finally collected my

thoughts. Pull yourself together Kobes, I said to myself. Ting-Ting's gonna show up here any second now. You don't have a choice. What you have to do right away is to wrap the whole discussion up as soon as humanly possible. My mind had prompted me to reach a quick compromise.

"Sure Shakes, of course." I said as graciously as I could. "After all, you said you liked her first. It's only fair. Go ahead, I'll try not to do anything that might diminish your chances in the meantime. Good luck!"

A massive wave of relief, appreciation and satisfaction came over Milkshake's face.

"Are you sure? Are you sure, Ko? Wow, thanks man, that's awesome!" he said, flinging the twig into a nearby rosebush. "I knew you wouldn't hate me if I asked you this!"

"Hate you? No way, dude." I smiled a Mr. Wu smile.

"You're a good guy, Kobi!" beamed Milkshake. "I knew I shouldn't stress about this. We've known each other too long." A great weight had been lifted from Milkshake's shoulders. He was all smiles.[4]

"No, no, c'mon." I said. "FCF, right?"

"For sure, man. FCF!" he replied, tapping me on the shoulder two or three times. "Thanks Kobi, you're the best! So...So, it's a deal, right?"

Milkshake held out his hand. I don't think we'd ever shaken hands before. It felt like I was signing a formal contract.

"Deal!" I said, giving his right hand a firm squeeze with my own.

I'd never seen my sharp-nosed friend so happy. So, of course, you're right, the worst thing that could possibly have happened then was for Ting-Ting to come walking up the road to my house at that very moment, shouting "Hi Kobi!" in her angelic voice. Unfortunately, that's exactly what happened.

註解

1   萊爾富 chain of Taiwanese convenience stores
2   片語：覆水難收 'water under the bridge'
3   萬里長城 literally 'thousand mile long city'
4   片語：滿面生花，眉開眼笑 'to be all smiles'

Art

藝

Chapter **15** / Still Wednesday Afternoon

What Comes First?

Ting-Ting and Milkshake hadn't spoken to each other since
the day of his fainting. In fact, Ting-Ting had avoided him
with so much instinctive skill that they'd hardly seen each
other at all. The smile on Milkshake's face gradually faded
as he turned around in great confusion. Ting-Ting appeared
equally shocked to see her not-so-secret admirer[1] right
there in front of her. It was the most awkward situation
imaginable, even more awkward than moments before. All
three of us wished we could shrink into little flakes of
dandruff and be scattered by the wind.

"Hey...Milkshake," Ting-Ting finally said, scratching her
perfect little elbow very self-consciously.

Milkshake—who's normally very prompt with any kind of
response—didn't reply for what felt like forever. I was
beginning to worry that the silence was going to balloon out
of control and swallow us all up.

"H...H...Hi Ting-Ting," he finally squeezed out between his
dry lips. "I'm here."

Milkshake obviously hadn't had enough time to rehearse
something cooler to say either. To his credit, it didn't take
him too long to recover and try to deal with the tricky
situation.

"Wh...wh what are you doing here?"

Milkshake had asked her this question in a very friendly tone but he rotated his coconut and pineapple head and flashed a very unfriendly glance in my direction. By the time he turned back, Ting-Ting had recovered too.

"Oh, I'm just here for an art project. Kobi was nice enough to let me paint Ro-Ro Gway-Gway," she said smiling sweetly at me.

"Wow, that really is very considerate of him," Milkshake said sarcastically[2] as he turned in my direction. I could swear he was looking around for something to throw at me. Another extremely long silence followed.

Just then, the one who was actually responsible for all of this, namely our star model Ro-Ro Gway-Gway the turtle, emerged from his afternoon soak in the saltwater[3] pool that Ye-Ye and I had built for him. Ting-Ting's face lit up like a disco ball when she caught sight of him.

"Wow, he's much bigger than I remember, Kobi! What have you been feeding him?" she asked enthusiastically.

Ro seemed to understand this because he raised himself up on his short thick legs as high as he could. Then he stretched out his wrinkled old mini-ostrich neck as far as it would go. Ting-Ting clapped her hands together excitedly.

"This is going to be my best sketch ever! Pleasssssseeee can we get started, Kobi?"

Ting-Ting didn't wait for a response. She'd already started making herself comfortable on a large smooth rock nearby, frantically digging away in her bag for some essential sketching equipment. In no time at all, she produced a whole range of stationery, the most prominent of which was a large pencil. She immediately started sharpening it very industriously. Ro was waiting patiently, rehearsing some of his best poses. Milkshake and I, for a moment both charmed by her vigor and enthusiasm, almost forgot that we were facing a much more severe problem than a broken Rubik's Cube. Our fascination with the gifted future art major didn't last long though. When Milkshake rotated his head this time, his eyes were as cold as ice. If he had cried at that precise moment, two glaciers would have run down his cheeks.

"I think I'll leave you two lovebirds alone now," he said with a sarcastic wink. Ting-Ting, however, found the composition of her magnificent model so stimulating that she hardly seemed to be aware of this comment.

"Shakes...hang on a minute," I said, trying to stop him as he turned away.

"No, no, Kobi. I'd hate to intrude. You guys do your thing. Don't mind me, you just take care of your lovely guest. Besides GCF,[4] right?"

He stared at me coldly like sheriffs stare at outlaws in cowboy movies. For a second, I honestly thought the way he was eyeing me was going to give me a bloody nose. Or burn through me like a laser.

"Shakes, it's not like that, I swear!"
"Whatever, man, spare me the trivial details," came the abrupt, almost simultaneous reply. The scorn and disappointment was evident in his indignant voice. "Hope you enjoy solo fishing."
Before I could stop him, Milkshake and his wounded pride had swung around and were storming off at a brisk pace in the direction of the beach. If he had challenged me to a fistfight to the death it would have been much easier to bear. Instead, he just left me standing there.
"Oh boy," I said to myself as I looked down at my lovely guest and the distant friend I wasn't going after. "This is not good."

At any other time I would have given sincere thanks to the universe for a chance to be alone with Ting-Ting, but I wasn't filled with gratitude now. Instead, I just felt really guilty. This was so unfair. Finally, I had the ideal excuse to be alone with the girl I'd had a crush on forever — in a place where no toilet paper was visible — and I couldn't delight

in it. Why was fate so cruel? What had I done wrong in my
previous lifetime?

"Do you want to watch, Kobi?" Ting-Ting asked without
looking up from the page.

Ro didn't move a muscle either; it was quite clear that he
was enjoying himself. Finally someone had realized how
incredibly sexy he was and was taking the time to dedicate
an entire artwork to him. Finally there was someone skillful
enough to accurately reproduce his sexiness on canvas.
While Ro took great pleasure in all this posing, I watched
Ting-Ting's tofu-colored hand flutter gently across the
page like a butterfly for a few minutes. The jade bracelet
she wore on her right wrist was tapping lightly on the
sketchpad. Like all great artists, she took her time. Slowly
but surely, a perfect copy of Ro's sexy turtle features was
starting to appear on the blank page.

"Finally someone had realized
how incredibly sexy he was..."

"Ting-Ting, why do you admire Ro?" I asked once the full outline of my best friend had emerged from the whiteness.

"Huh?" Again, the artist's eyes didn't leave her work.

"You said you had to sketch someone you admired."

"That's right."

"So?"

"So what?" The hand went on fluttering.

"So, why do you admire Ro?"

This time Ting-Ting did look up. She didn't say so, but I could see in her eyes that the answer to this question was as obvious as a lighthouse. And that I was a total EQ[5] idiot for asking. I had a hunch that if I dared to look over at Ro at that moment, his eyes would have said exactly the same thing.

Finally, she sighed. Even her sigh was beautiful! Then she blew some charcoal dust from the page and said (like someone explaining something to a small child), "Ro can travel. He can travel here, there, everywhere. All over the world if he wants to. Borders and nationalities don't apply to him. I envy him."

"Oh...?"

"I really do. And he doesn't have to say anything if he doesn't want to. People always expect us to say something, Kobi, it's such a nuisance. And we always feel like we either have to say something, or wait for someone else to. I hate it. It's exhausting. I admire Ro because he appreciates silence and doesn't always feel the need to chase it away. He has the ability to be quiet, despite what others expect of him. I wish I could do that."

Ting-Ting turned her head towards the sea and stared into the distance.

"Oh, and Ro doesn't need to eat fruit. I'm tired of people buying fruit all the time instead of growing it themselves. They're mere consumers. They don't produce anything. It's selfish and it's not very economical."

I did consider commenting on the fact that there were lots of animals that could be excluded from the 'need fruit' category, but I didn't want to ruin the moment. Also, I didn't really think of Ro as an animal.

I didn't respond for quite some time. Ting-Ting had lowered her head and was once more fully focused on her creation.

"He's my hero too," I said eventually, glancing over at the four-legged model.

Ting-Ting suddenly looked up at me and gave me her best smile. Finally I'd said something cool! I felt bad about breaking the silence and about buying fruit from Ting-Ting, but finally I'd said something cool.

"I know you love him a lot, Kobi. That's the only reason I haven't kidnapped him yet!" she said, still smiling.

Hearing Ting-Ting's perfect lips pronounce the word 'love' caused a warm blush to spread across my face, but luckily she didn't notice me glowing like a sky lantern. She was drawing again.

"Hey, Kobi, are you good at solo fishing? Oh, and what does GCF stand for?"

註 解

1　曝光的暗戀者 (詞彙 secret, admire)
2　諷刺地；挖苦地 (名詞：sarcasm，形容詞：sarcastic)
3　詞彙 saltwater=salt+water
4　Girls Come First 意味著女生比朋友還重要
5　情緒商數 Emotional IQ

Gold

金

Chapter **16** / ⭐⭐ ☁ Thursday

Teeth & Freedom

All this talk of admiration made me remember one of the people I admired most in the world. On Thursday afternoon after school, I decided to pay a visit to the local dentist, Dr. Qing.[1] He was another one of my more reliable consultants. Like Auntie Guo, he was always advising me on what to do. And what not do to. This time I needed some very important advice. Plus, I wanted to find out how long Ye-Ye still had to live.

Dr. Qing's assistant, Miss Chen,[2] was too busy crushing candy[3] on her smartphone[4] to notice me when I walked in, let alone offer any assistance. This problem of people looking down at their smartphones, while the world passes them by, has now reached epidemic proportions, I think. You hardly see anybody's eyes anymore! The only time you do is when they're mad at you and when they LINE you their latest picture. It's ridiculous.

Anyway, since Miss Chen was so distracted, I just strolled straight into Dr. Qing's office. I know privacy is a sacred thing, especially for people who aren't doing anything, but there was no time to lose. I found him behind his computer. This is where most doctors can be found these days. Ye-Ye says even health has been computerized.

Teeth & Freedom

"You can't just walk in here like you own the place, Kobi!"

"Don't worry, Doc, this is super important."

"Massive cavity in a top left molar?"[5] he asked, a little bit excited.

"Worse."

When Dr. Qing heard that the objective of my calling on him was to quiz him on Ye-Ye's expected lifespan,[6] he seemed a bit shocked.

"You know I'm only a dentist, right Kobi?" he asked hesitantly.

His complexion—normally exhibiting an abundance of blood—turned a little pale as he slowly removed his hands from the keyboard. Since founding his practice fourteen years ago, no patient had ever asked such a curious question.

Dr. Qing was a very modest person, even though everybody knew he was by far the most competent dentist in the whole county, maybe even in the whole country. Everybody also knew that he was the second most intelligent and rational person in town. (He was still trailing slightly behind Auntie Guo).

"Doctor, I know you know. I read somewhere that a person's mouth can tell you all about how healthy they are. They say a person's teeth should tell you their exact age. They say it's extremely accurate, like counting the rings in the sections of a tortoise's back or measuring the size of an Indian elephant's ears."

The dental expert raised his left eyebrow and folded his hands.
"You know your grandfather has false teeth, right Kobi?"
"So?"
"Well, if I'm correct, his false teeth are only five years old!" he declared with profound oral wisdom, looking at me with as if he'd just performed a highly complex calculation.
"Yep, five or six. I put them in myself. Did a wonderful job."
Just between you and me, it was this kind of unsatisfactory[7]

"I put them in myself.
Did a wonderful job."

reply that made me quite confident of one day overtaking Dr.
Qing in the official village intelligence rankings.

"You should get a pocket notebook like Da Vinci[8] and Auntie
Guo, Doc. You'll sound much smarter when you're requested
to diagnose patients' overall condition, or answer other
important questions."

Pacing around, I added with a little impatience, "You
know what I mean, Doc. Please! I have to...I have to start
planning..."

The dread in my appeal was evident. Dr. Qing's face suddenly
wore a very sad and meaningful frown that wrinkled his
entire intelligent brow.

"Come and sit down for a minute, Kobi," he said, crossing
his legs. Then he uncrossed them two or three times, as
if he were testing them, and finally decided not to cross
them at all. I sat down and found myself coping his awkward
movements.

Finally, when all four of our legs had at last come to a
complete rest, he looked into my eyes and pinched his nose
once or twice.

"In my opinion, Kobi," he said, "no young person should be
burdened with having to plan in advance for this sort of
thing. Or for these sorts of changes. Youth is much too

precious to waste on that. Also, no one should have to plan for something that's inevitable. You're far too young to worry about these sorts of things."

"Look, Doc, I'm not a child anymore. I'm nearly sixteen for goodness sake! I can cook." (Not really true.) "I know the difference between the Green Party and the Blue Party."[9] (Partially true.) "And, I can draw a pretty good diagram of bacteria when I need to." (True, if I concentrate.) "Why, I've nearly perfected my own signature for gosh sakes!" (I had spent a lot of time on that lately.) "Due to some recent developments, I might even have my first girlfriend soon." (Just to let you know, nothing actually happened between Ting-Ting and me yesterday, but I felt I needed to back up my statement with at least some sign of maturity to sound more convincing. Especially since I had no idea what 'inevitable' really meant.)

Mentioning political parties and a prospective girlfriend didn't seem as effective as I had hoped. Dr. Qing smiled at me the way most adults smile at adolescents who think they're nearly adults.

"Ye-Ye has an extremely healthy mouth for his age, Kobi," he said, gently rubbing his left temple with a steady hand.

"He gets plenty of exercise, so for his age, he's as fit as a fiddle. In addition to that, he eats lots of fresh fruit and vegetables. All of these lifestyle choices are highly beneficial and great for the immune system. If I'm not mistaken, he's never had any major surgery and he's not on any kind of medication either. On top of that, he's a very peaceful man, which, in my opinion, is far more effective in terms of longevity than being active or consuming mostly organic produce. Then, there's his very positive attitude— did I mention that? A positive attitude towards life makes a world of difference. Anyway, in the end, all of these factors need to be taken into consideration."

If they don't encounter any interruptions or objections, medical men have been known to go on like this for hours. I didn't have hours.

"Doc..." The tone of my voice implied enough impatience to make him cut straight to the conclusion.

"Anyway, in summary, Kobi my boy...nothing and no one is permanent. Not even artificial teeth, which, thanks to advances in modern technology and my skill, are just about as permanent as anything can be. But, barring serious injury, I don't see why he shouldn't live for many years to come."

I shook my head. "I think it's going to happen soon, Doc. I can feel it."

Dr. Qing remained in deep contemplation for a long time before answering. His eyes were serious but I could see all of his perfect teeth.

"Well, it's not like people have an expiration date, Kobi, so I'm afraid I really have no way of knowing."

"Where is he going after this, Doc?"

Dr. Qing paused for a long time before answering my question with one of his own. "Where do you think we go when we die, Kobi?"

"What?"

"You know, when we leave this physical realm..."

"Um, I'm not sure. Into the ground I guess. Is that right?"

"I can't give you a definite answer about this either, Kobi," said the dentist, "but, personally, I think it's more like through the ground."

"Through?"

"Yes, there's a subtle difference, Kobi. I believe you have a choice of where you want to go after you die, no matter what your beliefs are. Or were. The better person you are, the more choices you have. Some of us go through the ground, some go through fire, some through water and some through wood or gold.[10] Basically through all the things that keep you alive and that can kill you."

I didn't quite understand what the last sentence meant but the rest pretty much made sense. Maybe Dr. Qing had a little notebook in his pocket after all, I thought, looking out the window. When I turned back, his eyes were open but somehow it was as if he was far, far away. I think your eyes can leave this physical realm too when they want to.

Based on my own personal experience and what everyone I know says about him, your grandfather has been a good man throughout his whole life. Therefore, if he does leave us, you have no need to worry. Why? Because, he will have many, many choices of where to go next. Probably golden choices. Maybe when you die, you can choose to be with your grandfather again. Do you know what's special about choices, young man?"
"Is it that they can also kill us?"
The dentist opened his eyes and burst out laughing. He blinked several times before replying, "You are indeed no longer a child, Kobi!"

I was happy to hear him finally utter this admission, but I still wasn't a hundred percent sure if that was the right answer. Dr. Qing removed the handkerchief from his coat pocket and readjusted his glasses. He always did this when he had a desire to end the conversation. With the biggest smile I've ever seen on his face, he concluded.

"What's special about choices is that the more you have, the more freedom you have. Thanks to choices, Kobi, you can be free. And if you're free, young man, then you're happy. Even if you're dead. Never underestimate the value of freedom and how it affects our happiness. To come and go freely where and when you want to, is the key to being happy. Next time, make an appointment."

註 解

1　慶醫生 literally 'Qing Doctor'; Qing is a common family name
2　陳小姐 also Chan, common family name
3　指導智慧型手機和平板電腦玩的遊戲 Candy Crush Saga (糖果粉碎傳說) 'crushing candy' refers to Candy Crush Saga, a popular smartphone and tablet game
4　智慧型手機 (詞彙 smartphone=smart+phone)
5　臼齒
6　大限 , 生物的壽命 , 預期生命期限 (詞彙 lifespan=life+span)
7　不如人意 (詞彙 unsatisfactory=un (否定的)+satisfactory)
8　達文西　Leonardo da Vinci
9　民進黨 ; 國民黨 Two main political parties in Taiwan, namely the 'green' Democratic Party or DPP, and the 'blue' National Party or KMT.
10　五行 five ancient Chinese elements of which the entire universe is said to be composed, also the five phases of Chinese philosophy: 木火土金水 wood, fire, earth, metal, water

Red

紅

Chapter **17**　　⭐🌙　Friday. Saturday. Saturday Morning

Colors

The weekend had finally arrived. I was hoping Milkshake would have forgiven me by now and come over to fly kites or something. I waited around the house until it was nearly lunchtime but he didn't show up. To pass the time, I sat next to the pool and tried explaining the conversation I'd had with Dr. Qing to Ro-Ro Gway-Gway. He didn't look very interested. Being the fearless reptile that he was, he obviously didn't have to fret about dying or choices or any other philosophical stuff. Ro probably knew very clearly where he would be going one day anyway. Animals don't fool around, they always know. I'm sure they know where we're going too.

Since he seemed a bit bored, and since I didn't feel like a dip in the pool just yet, I asked him what I was going to do about Milkshake and Ting-Ting. This seemed to get his attention because he swam across to where I was sitting and made a splash or two with his flippers on the surface of the water. I knew the mention of Ting-Ting would probably cause some excitement, since the two of them really seemed to hit it off[1] the other afternoon. Yesterday at school, Ting-Ting gave me a color copy of her painting of Ro lying on the beach facing the ocean. Needless to say, I loved the creation just as much as I loved the creator. Miss Lin only gave her an A-minus, but love

had biased me against all professional opinion and to me it was
pure perfection.

My favorite part was the bottom right-hand corner where
she signed her name next to 'Toucheng[2] 2013'. Ye-Ye liked
it too, so we stuck it on the wall above the TV where some
of the cream paint was flaking. We didn't quite love it as
much as Ro did though; I caught him studying every inch
of his portrait whenever he was afforded an opportunity.
According to the Illustrated Guide to Marine Animals,
leatherbacks are one of the few sea creatures that can see
in full color. Come to think of it, Ro probably wasn't the most
objective person to ask for advice on that sensitive subject.

Time for a dip after all. As I plunged into the water, I was
pretty sure that the only two colors Milkshake was seeing at
the moment were red and green.[3] I decided that I'd have to go
to the drink shop in the afternoon and try to reason with him.
Try to make peace. He probably still wouldn't talk to me, but
at least it was less likely that he would beat me with a shovel
or throw something at me in public. Especially while he was
working. After that I had a gift that I wanted to take to Ting-
Ting at the fruit shop. You know—just to say thank you for the
drawing and all. And after that, I had to steal Officer Wang's

scooter and park it outside Brother Liao's house. It was going to be a busy day.

註 解

1　片語：一見如故 *'to hit it off with someone'*
2　頭城 literally 'head city'; small coastal town situated in Yilan County
3　片語：*'to see red'* 憤怒，很生氣，*'to be green with envy'* 非常嫉妒

Tea

茶

Chapter **18** / Saturday Afternoon

Foreign Chocolate, Ears and English

When I arrived at the drink shop there were several customers lining up for a Cantaloupe[1] & Chrysanthemum[2] Cocktail, the flavor of the week. How Milkshake ever managed to identify these two shapes from the rice in his lunchbox I'll never know, but we don't have time to get into that now. I joined the queue and waited patiently to get to the front. In my mind, I was rehearsing what I could say to my friend, like someone rehearsing checking in at an overseas hotel while waiting their turn to be served. Milkshake spotted me out of the corner of his eye but was determined not to let on that he had noticed me. This was going to be harder than I thought. Suddenly, I heard a strange voice over my left shoulder.

"Chocolate?" it asked.

Now, strange voices don't usually make me jump like a kangaroo, but this one was in English. Mr. Xu once told me that a cat has 32 muscles in each ear. Well, when I hear English, all the muscles in my ears—however many there are—immediately tense up like an elastic band. It's not that I hate the language, I just hate speaking it. As a result, whenever I see foreign surfers at the beach, I never have the courage to speak to them, even though they're always smiling and friendly. Why is it so easy to get embarrassed

when you're speaking a foreign language? I think it's
because you're worried that the other person will think
you're an idiot if you can't speak as fluently as they can. It's
actually so silly!

Anyway, back to the strange voice. I turned around slowly,
hoping to see a TV or something. Something that wasn't
speaking directly to me. Instead, I saw a large pair of
binoculars and an even bigger camera. When I lifted my
head I saw a plump white neck half covered by a big red
beard. I lifted my head a little more and finally saw a warm
spontaneous smile and eyes the color of olives. Oh no, not
a Lao-wai![3] Out of all the customers in the queue, he just
had to pick me, didn't he?! Why on earth was I so unlucky
these days?!

"Would you like some?" he asked again, holding up a large
bar of heavenly, cocoa-colored chocolate.
"Uh…"
"Ja, it's super tasty. Trust me. It's all the way from
Switzerland.[4] Exported. Or is imported? Anyway, snowy
mountain scenery and world-class watches—climbs and
clocks—that Switzerland."
He seemed very proud of the fact that it was all the way

from scenic Switzerland, so I couldn't really refuse. I was trying to remember if Switzerland was Sweden[5] or Sweden was Switzerland. I could never recall which one was always blanketed in more snow.

"Th...Thank you" I said, breaking off a small block and putting it in my mouth.

"Where I'm from in Switzerland, we say: "Danke Schön"[6] he replied. He was smiling wider than a harmonica until he placed a much larger chunk of chocolate in his own mouth.

He really was very friendly but his yellow teeth made me wonder how old he was, and how long he had to live.

"You try it, dan-kuh...schh-uhnn. Danke Schön!"

"Donkey...Sh...Shin.[7] How was that?" I asked timidly.

I couldn't help laughing at how strange the two words sounded compared to how he had said them.

"Ja, ja, outstanding!" he said. "Very good." He smiled again. "Ja, so far, I've never heard anyone say it better on their first try. If you just practice a little, you will sound Swiss in no time."

"You...you're a good liar, Mister," I said, also smiling broadly. "Danke Schön!"

I'd never had such delicious chocolate in all my life. Watch

Foreign Chocolate, Ears and English

out, Kobi, I told myself, there's no such thing as a free lunch.[8] Ye-Ye had told me how, a long time ago when he was boy, there were German missionaries in the town that used to offer him sweets whenever he was anywhere close to them. He told me that if you took the candy, you always felt like you had to go to church on Sunday. Then again, maybe foreigners just made friends with strangers by sharing their snacks. We do it, don't we? We're always showering foreigners with pineapple cakes and moon cakes and what have you. If foreigners leave Taiwan without having at least gained some weight, it's almost a national tragedy.

I tongued the chocolate around in my mouth very slowly. It really was very tasty.

"Do you think you can give me a hand, young man?" asked the Swiss gentleman.

I knew it! No such thing as a free lunch! So, he was spreading the gospel with chocolate, was he? It wasn't fair. Chocolate's such a powerful weapon. No teenager can resist it. Come Sunday I'd be sitting in the front row at church.

It was like he had read my racing mind because he looked quite amused.

"Uh...the menu," he said, smiling and raising his bushy eyebrows. He pointed to the large board above Milkshake's head. "It's all in Chinese."

"Oh...sure!" I said, turning towards the menu. So, that's all
he needed? I felt a bit bad. We're always so quick to judge,
aren't we? Well, I am anyway. It's such a bad habit.

I decided to start by translating the easiest words first.
"So, do you like green tea or red...I mean black tea?" I
asked.
"Green...sometimes...I think," he responded.
Grownups can be so ambiguous, can't they? They always
complicate things.
"With milk?"
 "Nein,"[9] he said, far more decisively this time. "Just black,
please. My doctor said I need to watch my cholesterol."
I had no idea what his doctor had told him to watch, so I
just smiled and nodded like a woodpecker. Then I started
scanning the rest of the menu on the wall.

"Oh, and it can't be too sweet either," he added, looking
down at the chocolate in his left hand. A few guilty
wrinkles appeared on his forehead as he contemplated this
secondary condition. For a second or two he looked like a
teenage truant whose hiding place was discovered by the
headmaster.
"My doctor said I shouldn't have too much sugar. She said

the Earth is on the verge of a carbon crisis and I'm on the
verge of a blood sugar crisis."

"Oh. Wow, Mister. That sounds...serious."

"Ja, she said I need to sort it out, because too much sugar
was like a cancer."

"Wow!"

"Ja, don't worry, my friend," he assured me. "I think she
said that just to frighten me. Like when she told me cola
was like acid. Or that I would die if I ate too many raisins!"
A very melancholy look flashed across the man's face.
That—and his belly of course—told me how well he and
sugary things had gotten along with each other in the past.

The melancholy didn't last though. Soon he seemed super
cheerful again.

"So, you really have to learn all those tiny little Chinese
characters by heart?" he asked, pointing at the menu again
and shaking his head.

I nodded mine.

"It really is quite incredible," he continued. "Now, reading
them I can understand, but *writing* them? Putting lots of
little lines the size of spider legs together to make words
like 'tea' and 'green' and 'milk'. Why, I cannot imagine it. It
really is quite marvelous! Native Chinese speakers must

have larger brains or something. I don't know where they keep them because their heads aren't really larger, but I'm sure they're bigger. Or maybe they're just heavier. Ja, I think one or two extra kilograms. Memorizing all those spiders. Ingenious!"

I wasn't completely sure what 'ingenious' meant, but he looked so jealous that I knew it had to be something good. Mr. Xu once told me that a spider has 48 knees.
"We have to study the words over and over again hundreds of times when we're young," I said, smiling shyly. "And I still make mistakes sometimes, to be honest."
"Ah, what modesty!" he replied. "Well, I think you're a genius, young man. And I can't believe your head is full of those characters and it's still smaller than mine. Much smaller. Unbelievable!"

I shook my much smaller head and smiled again, offering the following recommendation: "How about...green tea with passion fruit? I'll ask them not to add too much syrup." (I was extremely proud of myself for remembering the word 'syrup', by the way, and even allowed myself to daydream for one and a half seconds about being a translator one day.)
"Ja...sounds good!" he replied.

Foreign Chocolate, Ears and English

"Always large"

"Would you like a small, medium or large?"
He proudly tapped his big belly and said with a bigger
smile: "Always large."

He really was a very enthusiastic man. All at once his
eyebrows, tiny pink ears and large round belly rose up
a little higher. I'd never seen someone so happy at the
prospect of sipping on a cup of not so sweet passion fruit
flavored green tea.
"Danke Schön. Now I just need one more drink for my
daughter," he said.

Now, I didn't see anybody with him but like any normal
teenage boy, the sound of the word 'daughter' immediately

caught my attention. Those two syllables are usually enough to spur the curiosity of any young man.

"She likes milk tea a lot," he said, breaking off another block of chocolate. "Honey milk tea. As sweet as possible. And maybe they can throw in those strange little dark marbles[10] as well. Hannah loves chewing on the dark marbles."

"You mean pearl milk tea, right?" (Don't ask me how I remembered the word 'pearl' either. I was surprising myself this afternoon.)

Before he could reply, another strange voice, this time much younger and sweeter than a nightingale's, suddenly emerged over my other shoulder.

"Yes please, pearly milk tea!" it cried.

When I turned around, a beautiful fairy with long curly hair the color of a Vitali[11] can was standing in front of me. Her hair was so shiny that I was almost blinded. Her eyes were bluer than the sea. She was like something out of MTV.[12] You know, that place where everybody's impossibly slender, good-looking and energetic, and knows exactly how many calories are in everything edible. Daugh-ter.

She had a perfect face shaped like an upside-down pyramid and long, slim legs like a grasshopper. It was like meeting a

Foreign Chocolate, Ears and English

pop star or royalty! I guessed she was roughly the same age as me and Milkshake, but sometimes it's hard to tell with girls. Especially foreign girls.

"Ja, this is my beautiful daughter Hannah," said the man enthusiastically, pointing to the fairy with a proud father's finger.

Wow, she didn't resemble him at all! I thought to myself. That was a good thing. The father then raised the same proud body part to his left cheek, inviting a kiss with a tap or two. The young lady immediately obliged with a playful peck on the tapped cheek. The little golden cross and chain around her neck swung from side to side as she did so. Then, all of a sudden, she turned her splendid head towards me.

"Hi. I'm Hannah," she said, stretching out her hand. "H-A-N-N-A-H. If you start at the back it's spelt the same, so there's no way you can forget it!"

She giggled cheerfully.

"H...Hello Hannah," I said, shaking her soft, ivory hand. "My name's K...Kobi. K-O-B-I. If you start at the back you get... uh...never mind."

Hannah giggled even more.

Between you and me, I did consider tapping my cheek as well

like her proud pop had done—you never know!—but if she had kissed me I would probably have fainted like Milkshake did that day. Hannah. Cool name. Two syllables that were even better than the ones in daughter. And you could spell them either way! I suddenly felt that my name was highly inferior. Okay, I didn't have to tell these nice Swiss people that it was Haidi, but why couldn't I have a palindrome[13] for a name as well? Anyway, I really hoped that Hannah wouldn't notice how sweaty my palm was or how shaky my voice was. This was, after all, the first time I had ever touched a foreign girl's hand.

I was so busy being nervous that I didn't realize we'd reached the front of the line. Time flies when you're wondering what others think about you. We all turned to Milkshake. He was understandably a little shocked to see this strange combination of customers, but his business instincts soon took over.

"What can I get you?" he asked politely in Mandarin.

"Hannah, this is Milkshake. Milkshake, this is Hannah." I introduced them in English.

"Milkshake? That is the cutest name I've ever heard!" cried Hannah excitedly. I guess enthusiasm ran in the family.

Foreign Chocolate, Ears and English

Now, I've known Milkshake since we were kids, but I can honestly say that this was the first time I'd ever seen him blush.

"I chose it for him!" I said with a smile, trying to rescue my friend. "When he was young he liked to push and shove cows for no reason, instead of milking them, so I named him Milkshake."

The words had just left my mouth when I realized that they probably wouldn't help much to relieve Milkshake's embarrassment. However, at least the blonde's blue eyes shifted their focus to me instead for a brief moment, checking to see if this were true or not.

Unable to decide, she finally replied with a very broad smile, "Well, I love it!" Nice to meet you, Milkshake."

I then turned to her father, "And this, Milkshake, is...uh... sorry Sir, I don't know your name yet."

"Ja, I am Hans Kloss," he said confidently. "Photographer, astronomer, Asian antique dealer, newly appointed foreign diplomat and part-time lawyer. And amateur comedian!" he added with a big smile. "Nice to meet you too, Herr[14] Milkshake. I hear this is the best drink shop on the whole east coast!"

The compliment and the fact that he'd caught very little of

such an impressive self-introduction, only made Milkshake
even more embarrassed, especially since he didn't
understand how the east coast could have a hole in it.
With great effort, he nonetheless managed to squeeze out
a "S...sank you".

Poor Milkshake, it was as if his flip-flops[15] were glued to
the ground and his feet had been bound[16] together with
cables. His tongue was stuck to the roof of his mouth. He
couldn't stop staring at Hannah.

I'm afraid this condition didn't improve, even though Hannah
and Mr. Kloss had already started looking over the colorful
menu behind him. This was also the first time I'd ever seen
Milkshake frozen like a scarecrow. In fact, I was beginning
to worry that he had been permanently paralyzed and would
never be fully mobile again. Luckily, he jumped into action
automatically when I ordered a Passion Fruit Green (not
too sweet), a 'Pearl Pleasure' and a 'Flavor of the Day' in
Chinese. He still hadn't articulated a single sound apart
from the "S...sank you". However, there soon followed such
a deafening, industrial rattling of cups and ice cubes, and
such a banging open and shut of multiple refrigerator doors,
that I wondered for a second if there was a blacksmith or
a hippopotamus behind the counter. The rattling, banging,

manual stirring and mechanical blending continued for about four and a half minutes. Milkshake, having expertly completed his rapid rituals, then reappeared with a hop and a skip and three fabulous beverages.

Mr. Kloss looked suitably[17] impressed and started fumbling with a considerable amount of loose change in his pockets. "No, no. Over the house! No chargeee! No chargeee!" Milkshake declared with a big smile, placing on the counter the best Passion Fruit Green, Pearl Pleasure and Chrysanthemum & Cantaloupe Cocktail he'd ever poured. "Kobi, put these in a table for these nice people. Quic-ke. Quic-ke."
Milkshake had forgotten that the expression was 'on the house'[18] and that he never wanted to talk to me again, but he didn't care at all. Neither did I.

"Over the house!"

註解

1　哈密瓜 literally 'ha (as in ha ha) honey melon'

2　菊花

3　老外 literally 'old out'; colloquial term for foreigners

4　瑞士

5　瑞典

6　德文的謝謝 German for 'thank you'

7　驢子脛 donkey shin; 'shin' is the front of the lower leg.

8　諺語：天下沒有白吃的午餐 *'There's no such thing as a free lunch.'*

9　德文的不 German for 'no'

10　這位瑞士朋友提到的是放在珍珠奶茶裡面的珍珠，但是誤稱為彈珠遊戲用的彈珠 (marbles); refers to the tapioca balls found in popular Taiwanese drinks such as Pearl Milk Tea (詞彙：英文有一個較有趣的成語 'to lose one's marbles'，有發瘋或是失去理智的意思。'marble' 另外也有「大理石」的意思)

11　維大力 literally 'ties together great benefits'; popular Taiwanese soft drink sold in golden cans

12　詞彙 Music Television

13　回文

14　德文的先生 German for 'Mister' (Mr.)

15　拖鞋 literally 'drag shoes'; Chinese term also used for slippers and sandals

16　bind 過去式

17　適當地 (詞彙 suit 動詞 , suitable 形容詞)

18　片語：免費 , 免錢 *'on the house'*

Risk

險

Chapter 19 / Saturday Evening

A Risky Mission Starts

I hung out at the drink shop with Mr. and Miss Kloss the whole afternoon. They both had very lively personalities and were very talkative. I'd never spoken so much English in my whole life. In-between smiles and sips, we chatted about this and that. I didn't understand everything they said, and I was hardly fluent, but for the first time in my life, it didn't matter.

All evening during his shift, Milkshake dashed back and forth bringing us all kinds of fantastic tea flavors to sample. Soon, we'd all had so much to drink that none of us were particularly thirsty, but there was no way we could refuse. By now, Milkshake had made a miraculous recovery from his initial embarrassment. When there weren't any other customers, he even joined us and spoke far more English than I ever remember him learning. For someone who had difficulty reciting the alphabet, he was being awfully sociable.

It turned out that Mr. Kloss was just on holiday. He'd be catching the bus back to the airport in a couple of weeks. He said he'd put off his return to Switzerland once or twice already because he liked Asia so much, but that he couldn't allow any further delays. He joked that any more postponements and his wife, Hannah's mother, would break his nose with a bread knife.

Hannah, on the other hand, was actually an exchange student. She was going to be in Taiwan for a whole year. Milkshake made a vain attempt to hide his extreme happiness at hearing this arrangement, but it was painfully obvious. Like me, he wasn't a great actor. It was love at first sight and he'd forgotten all about Ting-Ting. On top of that, he'd even forgiven me for having once liked the same girl as he did. Forgetfulness isn't always such a bad thing after all.

The best part was that Hannah seemed to like him too. Well, put it this way, I don't think there was any danger of her getting homesick just yet, or feeling lonely when her dad went back to Switzerland. Know what I mean? Wink wink ;-).

Things were, in fact, going so smoothly today that I even started to feel a bit more confident about stealing a policeman's scooter later that evening. I'd won back Milkshake's trust by introducing him to a blonde beauty. Things were back to normal. I even considered recruiting him for the dangerous mission that lay ahead. However, in the end, I decided that I didn't want to drag him in as well, just in case things went horribly wrong. If I liked the same girl as him and got him into jail in the matter of a week, that really would be going a bit too far. Friendships can only handle so much, you know.

So, after Mr. Kloss and Hannah returned to their
guesthouse[1] for the evening, and after I teased Milkshake
a little for falling in love with a foreigner (he loved every
minute), I slowly made my way to the Wang residence.
The house was on Octopus Avenue. As I walked along, my
stomach was all twisted in a knot and it felt like there was
a big fat frog stuck in my throat. Nerves. Don't you hate
nerves? Being nervous is like sitting on the back of a wild
rhinoceros; you're awake and fully conscious, but you're not
really in control. I'm not exaggerating. Anyone who has ever
stolen a police scooter will know exactly what I'm talking
about. No matter how hard you try, your mind just goes
wherever the nerves go. At the moment, they were heading
straight for being shot or being imprisoned. Oh, by the way,
if you catch anyone purchasing a product made from rhino
horn, you should arrange for them to trespass on a certain
person's vegetable garden. Wink wink ;-)

As I turned onto Octopus, I saw two elementary school
kids coming down the road. One was bouncing a rubber ball
on the asphalt.[2] The other was playing with her diabolo,[3]
which wasn't good for my nervous stomach. They hardly
noticed me as they passed. Once they were well out of sight,
I paused and took a pair of bright purple dishwashing gloves

and a big floppy[4] hat out of my jacket pocket. I snatched the
gloves from their usual spot next to the kitchen sink. I don't
usually wear hats — they don't suit me — but I borrowed one
of Ye-Ye's gardening hats for the mission. For the record, I
don't usually sport purple dishwashing gloves either, but I've
watched enough movies and detective shows to know about
fingerprints[5] and all that stuff.

From the other jacket pocket, I produced one of those
cheap 20 NT[6] gray facemask[7] you can buy at any Seven.[8] As
I pulled out the mask, something dropped onto the ground.
I stooped to pick it up. Oh boy. I'd forgotten all about the
present for Ting-Ting! Remember? I was planning to drop it
off at the fruit store earlier. Anyway, I quickly replaced it
and decided that I'd drop by there the following day instead.
Well, if I wasn't in prison, of course. There was no way I
could see Ting-Ting now. I was already sitting on the back
of a wild rhino. I didn't want to make it angry as well. For
the first time, it crossed my mind that I'd never see Ting-
Ting again if I was detained, convicted and sentenced to
spend the rest of my life behind bars.[9] Plus, the harsh reality
was that she'd probably never want to speak to me again if I
was a criminal. Luckily,
I didn't have time to worry about that now, otherwise I
might have started sobbing like a little baby.

Hat...check. Gloves...check. Mask...check. The disguise was complete. I also changed into some darker clothes earlier before going to the drink shop. I had on a navy sweater and dark blue jeans. I can't say I like wearing jeans; they tend to restrict your movements. Like everyone, I guess criminals have to make sacrifices. All in all, I was as ready as I could be. I was wearing every article of clothing necessary to perform an innocent robbery. My first criminal outfit.

Having transformed my appearance into one more suitable for this kind of venture, I proceeded with great caution. Slowly but surely, I drew closer and closer to number eighty-three. I was like a leopard stalking its prey on tiptoe. Funny, I was wearing all this disguise gear and stuff, but it felt like everyone could see me as clear as day. At least they probably wouldn't know who I was though. I reckoned if something went wrong and the Wangs did notice me outside their house, they wouldn't recognize me at all.

When I reached the white baseball shaped mailbox[10] with a large '8' and '3' on it, I stopped. The lights were burning inside. I could hear one of those Taiwanese cooking shows coming from the TV in their living room. "*Add the onion and garlic first. Then the baby shrimp. Then...*" Mrs. Wang's silver Toyota was parked outside on the street in front of their gate. I looked around for Officer Wang's police scooter. To my utter dismay, I saw it standing inside the yard next to Mrs. Wang's pink bicycle with the purple basket. The scooter was facing the house. Oh no! Now I'd have to open the gate and slip inside to get to the scooter. The huge element of risk involved with this made my blood run cold. 'Courage, Kobi, courage!' I tried to tell myself. 'At least they don't have a big fierce dog that would rip you to shreds as soon as you opened the gate.' Well, not that I knew of anyway.

Another chief concern was that the gate would be rusty. That would mean that it would creak and whine when I opened it. I didn't want to risk that, to be honest. Mr. & Mrs. Wang's ears had supernatural powers. They were especially trained to detect naughty adolescents and bad citizens. At the moment, I was being both, so I had to be extra careful. There was no way I could get away with making even the slightest noise. I would have to be as quiet as a mouse, or else it would all be over in an instant. My hand was trembling as I reached for the iron bolt on the gate...

註 解

1 民宿 (mínsù) (詞彙 guesthouse = guest + house)
2 柏油 (詞彙 tar)
3 扯鈴 also called a Chinese yo-yo
4 鬆軟的 , 下垂的
5 指紋 (詞彙 fingerprint=finger+print)
6 台幣 NT$ (New Taiwan Dollar) currency of Taiwan
7 口罩 (詞彙 facemask=face+mask)
8 7-ELEVEN (7-11) convenience store
9 片語 : 被關押 , 坐牢 , 在監獄服刑 *'to be behind bars'* (詞彙 behind, bar)
10 郵筒 , 信箱 (詞彙 mailbox=mail+box)

Collide

撞

Chapter **20** / Saturday Evening

Seconds later. A Risky Mission Continued...

This was scarier than a midnight cemetery. The gate and the walls at the back, surrounding the yard, felt as high as skyscrapers. Every nerve in my body was cautioning me against going any further. All I wanted to do was to run back home and forget about the whole thing. I don't know why, but that's not what I did. Instead, I very delicately lifted the bolt using only my right thumb and index finger.[1] Then, I carefully slid it to the side. After taking two deep breaths, I swung the gate open very gently. I was super relieved to find that it didn't make a sound. Leaving the gate slightly open, I slipped into the yard, keeping low and treading very lightly. As I edged closer to the scooter, I noticed a white helmet hanging on the right handlebar. The keys were in the ignition![2] Oh, thank goodness! Now at least I wouldn't have to break into a policeman and principal's house to snatch the keys for the scooter I was going to steal. That would be verging on insanity. Bordering on madness. Or suicide — take your pick.

The keys were a sign, I thought to myself. A sign to go ahead! But, just as I was beginning to feel a little optimistic about the outcome of this whole adventure, something happened that made me freeze in my boots. My tiptoes were just about to reach the blue and white scooter,

when I heard Mrs. Wang's voice suddenly rising above the
professional cooking advice coming from the TV.

"Hey...Laogong![3] You forgot to close the gate again, you
absentminded old baboon!"[4]
"Huh?" I heard Mr. Wang enquire from the other side of the
room.
"Yeah, I don't know what I should be more worried about, my
darling donkey. Your memory...or your eyesight!"
I turned round just in time to see a hand brush the lounge
curtains aside. As I quickly ducked behind the police scooter,
Mrs. Wang's eagle eyes appeared at the window. They were
focused on the open gate.
"Stop changing the channel and come and see for yourself if
you don't believe me, Pigeon-Brain!" she said.
Then she started waving some expensive kitchen utensil
in the direction of the gate. Like all good wives, she loved
pointing out her darling husband's blunders with sophisticated
kitchenware.

The gesture produced the desired result because, moments
later, an annoyed Officer Wang made a reluctant appearance
at the glass as well.
"That's very strange," he remarked, scratching the short

shaven hair above his big right ear. "I could have sworn I closed it when I came in earlier."

"Well, you must be getting old, dear," replied Mrs. Wang.

"Humph," Officer Wang snorted in response.

I heard the lock of the door open. My entire body was frozen. Then came Mrs. Wang's voice again: "Hang on! You might as well throw out the garbage while you're at it."

Like all good wives, she'd also mastered the art of giving her husband instructions.

There followed some more male mumbling and rustling inside. Half a minute later, the kitchen door swung open and a very irritable policeman stepped out carrying a large black trash bag. My heart was in my mouth. 'This guy's going to kill you if he sees you, Kobi! You're going to end up in one of those bags!' I told myself. He was really close. Thank goodness it was already getting dark and he hadn't turned on the outside light in the yard. Still, if he turned to his left he would definitely be able to see me squatting behind the scooter. I remained perfectly still, hardly breathing.

Just when I thought things couldn't get any worse, I heard Mrs. Wang's voice rise up again. "I'll turn the light on for you, dear, we can't have you fooling around in the dark out

Seconds later. A Risky Mission Continued...

there. Sometimes I think you really should still be wearing a diaper."

Officer Wang tried to protest that he wasn't blind or a baby, but, seconds later, the light in the yard went on. A big, broad naughty-detecting beam of light illuminated the entire place. I was in a real pickle now. Done for. My life was over. Prison, here I come. All I could do was pray, and brace myself for the worst...

The only thing that saved me was that Mr. Wang was too busy taking out the trash to turn to his left just yet. He was also distracted by fantasies of divorcing his wife. I could hear him mumbling to himself about how she was always helping him when he didn't need help. Thank goodness he had such a fragile ego! It gave me a few precious seconds to remind myself not to panic and to figure out where to hide. I looked around quickly. To my horror, there was absolutely nothing else in the yard apart from one or two gardening tools and a handful of foot-high, freshly watered bonsais.[5] Ugly, deformed[6] bonsais. I made up my mind to mumble to myself about this rotten luck later, but this was not the time for complaining. This was the time for action.

So, I did the only thing I could do. I positioned myself behind the police scooter and curled myself up into as small a ball as possible. Like an armadillo.[7] Then, I started praying that someone or something divine would suddenly decide to make me transparent. Or, give me legs like a locust so I could clear the wall with one single, decisive dive. As I sat there hunched up into a tight little armadillo bundle, I could feel the anxiety gripping my whole body. I could swear Mr. Wang could hear my lungs hastily expanding and contracting in my chest. Mr. Xu once told me that ants don't have any lungs. Good time to be an ant.

Officer Wang slowly progressed to the garbage can and placed the black bag inside. Then he strode over to the gate, still muttering to himself. He was just about to close it when I had a sudden inspiration. I wasn't eating rice at the time,[8] so I honestly don't know where it came from, but I had it all the same. I silently searched through the contents of my trouser pockets and located some spare change I had left from the drink shop. Seventy-seven NT. Altogether, there were eight coins of different sizes. It wasn't a large sum of money, but I suddenly realized that it could buy my escape. Could it work? I was desperate—it had to work.

There was no time to hesitate. I stood up very slowly. Then I put my left foot forward, bent my knees slightly and raised

Seconds later. A Risky Mission Continued...

my cupped right hand containing the coins. Steadying myself, I took one or two practice swings. All the while, I took great care to make sure that the coins didn't shake like a piggybank in my gloved hand. Mr. Wang had slid the bolt back into position and was just about to turn back towards me. His murmurs were getting louder. I took a deep breath through my nose, drew my right arm into my side, aimed for the streetlamp on the left opposite the Wang's gate, and closed my eyes. Then I said a silent prayer and finally launched the batch of coins high into the night sky...

It felt like forever before I heard a distant jingle of coins crashing onto the asphalt road and concrete sidewalk. They'd all landed somewhere in the vicinity of my target. I opened my eyes to see Officer Wang now also frozen on the spot. His eyes were fixed on the ground. His head was tilted slightly in the direction of where the unexpected sound had come from. It seemed as if every single cell in his body was wide awake and alert. What had been the cause of the sudden noise? I could smell his police brain working overtime. As swift as a little sparrow, the officer jumped around quick as popcorn and reached for the gate.

"Anybody there?" he said, removing the latch cautiously. Then he froze again and waited.

When, after a few seconds, the only forthcoming reply came from the TV inside, he opened the gate and stepped out into the street. Again he stopped in his tracks, suspiciously looking up and down the road. Having to admit to himself that he'd firstly left the gate open, and was now hearing strange noises made by invisible people in the street, put Officer Wang in an even more dreadful mood.

"If I find you kids, there'll be triple trouble!" he said firmly. Then he expertly surveyed every possible hiding place that existed within a radius of 20 meters.

"Even if I have to patrol the whole street for the whole night...I will find you! The Law shall prevail!"

When this warning was not followed by any naughty giggling or stirring, or any other notable signs of mischief, Officer Wang finally sighed and advanced to where the coins lay scattered in the street. Through the gate, I saw him bend down to perform a thorough inspection of the 77 NT that had mysteriously rained down from the sky. Soon, Officer Wang seemed completely occupied with examining the coins. He was even smelling one or two of them. He put one on his tongue. The cause of their appearance was consuming his senses.

Seconds later. A Risky Mission Continued...

I realized that the time had come to make my second move.
The wave was slowly rising up in front of me. Now was
the time to turn around and start paddling! If I missed this
golden opportunity to catch my wave to freedom, there
would indeed be triple trouble. In one fluid motion, I hopped
onto the scooter and turned the key clockwise. I pressed
the starter button with my thumb and held it there. Then,
with a flick of my right wrist, I rotated the accelerator. The
engine came to life. It roared once or twice like a wild animal
about to break out of a cage. I looked up and saw Principal
Wang's hand once again disturbing the curtains. 'Where is
that baboon of a husband off to now, at this late hour?' she
was probably asking herself. Her husband was at that very
moment wondering the exact same thing about his wife.
"Laopo?"[9] I heard him ask in astonishment as he turned
round to face the gate.
"Where are you going?"
There was no time to lose. Movie stunt time.

Turning the accelerator hard this time, I sped off aiming for
the open gate. It was like the police scooter had been fired
from a cannon. The white helmet went flying off to one side,
smashing into a drainpipe.[10] Wild animals are quite tough
to control, you know, especially if you're wearing ridiculous

purple dishwashing gloves. I didn't seem to be going where I was aiming. First, I collided with an ugly bonsai or two. I think this improved their appearance. Then, I hit the purple bicycle basket. Then the white helmet I'd sent crashing to the ground moments earlier. I was so nervous that I burst out laughing. I couldn't help myself. Here I was trying to make the perfect getaway and instead I was hitting just about every single object in the Wang's yard. It was like things were just jumping out of nowhere and they were hitting the scooter! And still, I kept giggling to myself!

Somehow, by some miracle, I had kept my balance. The yard was in ruins and my stomach ached from all the laughing, but I kept my balance! It wasn't pretty but—don't ask me how—I managed to bounce my way through the gate, down the sidewalk and into the empty street. The last thing I hit on my way out was the gigantic baseball. I hit that so hard that it cracked like an egg, spraying out advertising leaflets and one or two unpaid electricity bills. Just about the only thing blocking my way that I had successfully avoided, was Officer Wang himself. Since I started my little tour of destruction through the yard, he'd left the spot where the coins had landed and taken a few tentative steps towards the gate. He was now close enough to see that the destructive rider was not his Laopo.

Seconds later. A Risky Mission Continued...

"What?!" he cried out in complete disbelief as I shuttled
past him at breakneck[11] speed.

He stretched out a hand and snatched at me instinctively. He
missed. I was still giggling into my gray facemask as I turned
sharply to the right, leaving behind me a thick trail of dirty
blue scooter fumes.

Hysterical screams of "Hey you!" "Freeze!" "Come back!"
"Thief! Crook!" "Intruder!" and "Stop himmmm!" followed
me all the way down Octopus Avenue. It felt like even
the screams were snapping at my heels. The last thing I
remember hearing was: "the Law shall prevailllll!"

Then, it was as if my criminal mind (didn't know I had one)
took over. 'Speed up, Kobi!' it said. I obeyed. The terrifying
thought of the scooter breaking down finally brought an end

"He missed."

to my giggles. And what if the owner gave chase on his wife's bicycle?! Or what if he caught up to me with that long reach of his and those giant bamboo-leg strides?! 'Faster Kobi!' it said. I obeyed again.

I headed west as fast as I could and didn't dare look back to see if anyone was in pursuit or not. I didn't even dare turn my head. It was only after around eight or nine minutes of supersonic speeding through a blur of narrow, winding farm roads and dark alleys, that I realized I wasn't being pursued by anyone. I could now seriously consider braking for the first time. I gradually slowed down, looking over my shoulder once or twice. There was no one there. I'd gotten away from him. I eventually came to a complete stop at a fork in the road. To the left, was an abandoned wheat field. Behind it, I could just make out the dark outline of a local steel factory. To the right, was a single lane bridge over a small stream.

Turning my head around frantically in all directions, I listened very carefully for any sign of a threat. I felt like a robber who's just robbed an ATM[12] and is waiting for the bank security guards to catch up. I must have stood there for at least two minutes, almost too afraid to breathe in case it made too loud a noise. I could hear a gentle breeze

Seconds later. A Risky Mission Continued...

rustling through the leaves in the quiet night air. The occasional cricket chirping or dog barking somewhere in a distant residential area were the only other things that broke the silence. These familiar, ordinary sounds of the night helped to calm my nerves. I finally released my iron grip on the bike's handles and uncurled my fingers once or twice. They felt stiff and hard. I took off one of the absurd purple gloves and squeezed it a few times with my bare hand. I couldn't help smiling at how many things I'd collided with in the yard. You're lucky to be here, Kobi, I thought. I ran my fingers through my hair and took three deep breaths. Breathe in—a chirp. Breathe out—a bark. Rustle, rustle, rustle. Calm. Calm. Calm. Suddenly, my entire body felt ice, ice cold. I shivered and noticed a strange internal discomfort in my bowels. Ye-Ye's hat was no longer on my head.

註 解

1 食指 literally 'food finger'

2 點火開關 literally 'start fire switch'

3 老公 literally 'old male'; informal term for 'husband', similar to 'hubby'.

4 狒狒

5 盆栽

6 不成樣子，變形的 (詞彙 deformed=de+form; 參考 defect, decrease, deter)

7 犰狳

8 參考第三章 like Milkshake does when he has new ideas; see chapter 3

9 老婆 literally 'old woman'; informal term for 'wife'

10 詞彙 drainpipe=drain+pipe

11 非常危險的 , 極快的 (詞彙 breakneck=break+neck)

12 詞彙 automatic teller machine

Whale

鯨

Chapter **21** / Sunday Morning

Guilty Stomachs and Successful Invitations

The sun was streaming in through my window when Ro woke me up the next morning. He was tugging at my quilt with his toothless beak. I opened my eyes slowly and held my breath under the covers. The previous night's events started coming back slowly but surely into my mind. Was it all a dream? No. It was very real. Had anyone witnessed the crime and exposed me? Was I in jail? No again, I was at home. Relief. Was there a flock of inspectors waiting to question me at the foot of my bed? Waiting to make the arrest? I didn't hear anyone. More relief. Was Ye-Ye standing over me with the Antenna of Justice? (The Antenna of Justice was a broken old radio antenna that he would smack my bottom with when I was being naughty. Like when I stole scoops of ice cream out of the fridge before dinner, or when I filled the sugar bowl with salt.) No, I didn't feel anyone smacking me. Okay. I finally breathed out, pulled back the covers and sat up in bed.

Ro was staring up at me with his wise, dark eyes. There was no one else in the room. True, I had come back minus a hat but...maybe, just maybe, I could get away with this.
"I think it might have worked, Handsome!" I said, smiling down at my best friend. "Looks like we can set aside all those disturbing visions of capture, trial and imprisonment

Guilty Stomachs and Successful Invitations

for the moment, hmm?"

Ro blinked a few slow motion turtle blinks. I knew what
he was thinking. He was thinking that, yes, he was indeed
handsome. He was also thinking that the idea of being
associated with juvenile delinquents who violated other
people's constitutional rights, didn't really appeal to him.
In fact, it was obvious that Ro didn't approve of my actions.
He wouldn't have an ounce of sympathy for me if I spent
the rest of my life in a cold dark cell, warmed only by the
memory of him. He was also thinking that my quilt tasted
like old socks.

Once he was satisfied that I'd sufficiently read his mind, he
flicked his wrinkly head back and started sliding towards
the front door. He was intent on distancing himself from
the criminal immediately, just to reinforce his point. My
eyes followed him out the door and then looked up at the
ceiling. I recalled the previous night's events in more detail.
All in all, there had been seventy-nine casualties during the
completion of the mission. Seventy-seven of those were NT
dollars. One was an oversized baseball. One was a hat. If
it weren't for the latter, I would have said that the mission
had gone pretty well. I parked Officer Wang's scooter right
outside Brother Liao's house, like I told Mr. Wu I would, and

made it all the way home without being noticed by anybody. Well, I don't think anybody noticed me. What was that idiom about chickens that can count before they hatch?[1] Can't remember. Anyway, I know it means you should never celebrate too early.

Oh, whether or not Brother Liao had then parked the scooter under a truck somewhere in his sleep, as he was supposed to, I had no idea. Whatever the case may be, there was no way Mr. Wu could say I hadn't fulfilled my end of the bargain. To tell the truth, I was even a little proud of myself for having been so courageous and strategic the night before. Maybe even a little creative. I soon forgot about how I was praying and shaking in my boots most of the time.

Two big questions remained. One, where had Ye-Ye's hat ended up? And two, could the person who found it, identify it as belonging to Ye-Ye? Oh, one more thing, did Ye-Ye know I had borrowed his hat?
The answers to these questions weren't in the sea, but that's where I went to look for them.

When Ro and I had finished our surf, I dragged him back up the beach on the Ro-Mobile. I had a quick shower outside

Guilty Stomachs and Successful Invitations

and then stormed into the kitchen with a towel around my waist. It was time for breakfast. The activities and the tension of the night before, as well as the morning's exercise, had taken their toll. I was as hungry as a wolf. When I reached for my second steamed bun—after having already finished two bowls of cereal with soymilk—and started devouring it as if it had featured as the main attraction of some royal banquet, Ye-Ye finally raised a bushy white eyebrow. He put down the newspaper he'd been thumbing through very serenely up to that point.

"Ok, Kobi, what did you do?" he asked very calmly.

Nearly choking on my steamed bun, I looked up in surprise.

"C'mon, spit it out, my boy" he said with a knowing smile.

"This is a very interesting article about the dangers of caffeine, and I'd like to get back to it."

"Huh?" was all I could manage, steamed bun fragments flying everywhere.

"Kobi, Kobi, Kobi..." continued Ye-Ye, shaking his head, "the last time you were dying of starvation, my boy, was when you knocked over Nai-Nai's favorite vase with your surfboard and blamed it on your turtle."

"But...I..."

"It's the guilt, you see. It's really very good for the appetite. People try to cover up their guilt with food. It never works but that's what they do. My father always told me that guilt makes you greedy. Maybe that's why he was so skinny. In fact, he was an innocent skeleton of a man. Sure, his moods, opinions and outlooks were all as changeable as the weather, and he loved whining about this and that, but I can tell you here and now, there was not a guilty bone in his body!"

Of course I was doing absolutely everything I could at that moment to look more skinny and less guilty, but I wasn't sure it was working.

"Uh...I think I'm just growing, Ye-Ye."

That was the only adequate explanation I could come up with just then. I was finding it hard to maintain eye contact with my grandfather.

Ye-Ye smiled as if his gums could absorb all the truth floating around in the air. As he disappeared behind his newspaper once more, he said, "Don't worry, my boy," like a triumphant psychologist that knew everything. "You can tell me all the details regarding the mischievous matter when you bring my hat back. I'm sure I have a spare lying around somewhere."

The last sentence cut through me like a lightning bolt and, in a flash, transported me back to the night before. I hated

Guilty Stomachs and Successful Invitations

lying to Ye-Ye. I knew how much it disappointed him because Ye-Ye himself hated lying. A dishonest tongue was the only thing in life that he truly despised. He always used to say that lies were like plastic—they seem useful at the time, but in the end they just make a mess that never dissolves.
(I think he meant the mess never biodegrades[2] but...well... you know.)

When I was eleven, Ye-Ye told me that if you lie you can't forget the truth. And if you can't forget the truth, then you can't sleep at night. Like when you forget your baggage on the station platform. Or when you regret doing something that you shouldn't have done. I was only eleven at the time so it took my brain a few months to process what he said (and to forget about the imaginary lost luggage), but in the end I had to agree. To keep remembering the truth could only give you nightmares. That's why honesty is such an invaluable asset.

The worst part was that Ye-Ye would never punish me if he knew I'd lied to him. Some parents or guardians will hit you with a cane or an old pair of slippers, or an Antenna of Justice, if they find out you lied to them. They'll hit you till your bum looks like a sunburnt zebra's. Some won't hit you but they'll forbid you from playing video games[3] or something like that. Or, they'll ground you for a week. Some take away your allowance. Ye-Ye didn't do any of those to deal with liars. For him, punishment for dishonesty was all psychological. This was much worse. Not only because it hurt more, but also because, after a while, you start punishing yourself! So cunning! You can run away from armed people in a rage like Mr. Wu, or from people who love dealing out physical punishment like Mr. and Mrs. Wang, but you can never run away from yourself. No one is that fast.

I wasn't hungry anymore. I left Ye-Ye with his newspaper and stepped outside again. I suddenly had an idea. I don't know why, but somehow I was sure that Ting-Ting would know what to do. I was convinced that she'd make an accurate assessment of the situation and be able to offer some advice. Maybe it's just that people in love have a tendency to believe that the person they're in love with, can fix anything. In any case, I still wanted to drop off her gift. I decided to set out for the fruit shop right then and there. I wasn't sure this time if it was the universe or myself that was giving me another ideal excuse to see her, but to be honest, I didn't really care anymore.

Guilty Stomachs and Successful Invitations

When I arrived there at around eleven o'clock, the season's first durians[4] were being displayed at the front of the shop in all their spiky glory. Nai-Nai had taught me at an early age how to peel durians—keeping my blood in my body—and stash[5] them in the freezer as a yummy natural ice cream. They were perfect for those hot spring and summer days. Whenever I saw those golden brown spikes, I thought of Nai-Nai. Maybe she was still floating around in her little boat somewhere, who knows? Just like that guy from India in the story with the seasick[6] tiger. [7]

Ting-Ting, as usual, was as busy as a bee. She was giving the floor a quick sweep and arranging some of the empty cardboard boxes at the back of the shop. She smiled when she looked up and saw me poking out from behind the spikes. "They're not quite ripe yet, Kobi. I'm afraid you'll have to wait one or two more days. Then they'll be just right. These little yellow watermelons should be fine though. They taste super sweet, trust me," she said, gently tapping one or two with her fingers. Shall I ask my little brother to help you choose one? I swear he can taste with his hands or something, because he always knows which one is the sweetest."
Mr. Xu once told me that butterflies taste with their feet.

At the time, I wanted to reply that Ting-Ting's feet were as pretty as a butterfly, but I didn't.

"Ah...no thanks, Ting-Ting," I said, nearly bumping into the durian display.

"Actually, I...I just wanted to..."

"Hey, did you hear about Officer Wang's scooter? They towed it out of the water in the harbor this morning!" she interrupted.

"The harbor?!" I looked at her in amazement.

"Yep. Apparently, that's where Brother Liao parked it last night! Ha! Ha! Right next to a big, fat expensive yacht!" Ting-Ting laughed. "My mom heard all about it at the hairdresser this morning."

"Wow, but..."

"Oh, don't worry, Kobi, there were no casualties. Everyone's fine. But the bike has to be scrapped, of course."

"Did you hear about Officer Wang's Scooter?"

Guilty Stomachs and Successful Invitations

A beauty parlor is a very reliable source of information, by the way. As dependable as a rice cooker. You can bet your bottom dollar that everything Ting-Ting just said was really true.

"Really?" my throat was a bit dry.

"It's true alright, Kobi, the hairdresser wasn't just making it up. Apparently, it's all over the headlines in the county papers."

"Papers?"

"Yep. Apparently some have nice color pictures of the dripping scooter hooked up to a tow truck and everything! Isn't it the funniest thing you've ever heard?"

I attempted an appropriate level of real laughter in response to this, but I don't think it sounded very genuine.

"Crazy, right?" she continued. "That Brother Liao is something else! A complete lunatic!"

I know she meant that in a nice way. Brother Liao was a fellow artist after all. Plus, her eyes were gleaming as if she thought it was the most impressive and creative bit of parking she'd ever heard of.

"Anyway...Sorry, Kobi, what were you saying? What can I get you?"

I was relieved that the topic had changed so swiftly.

"Uh, actually Ting-Ting, I just wanted to give you something."
Ting-Ting tried to conceal her curiosity, but her raised eyebrows betrayed her. She wiped her hands shyly on her apron and stepped out from behind the counter, still smiling.

"My birthday's only in July and Christmas is in December, Kobi," she remarked playfully, once she'd moved a little closer. "Don't you think you're a little bit early?"
"Oh, in that case I'll come back in July." I replied, half turning around.
Ting-Ting rolled her eyes and laughed. "Early's good! Early's good!" she said, by now dying of curiosity.
I made her wait a little longer before finally reaching into my pocket and producing the small item that I'd nearly lost the night before on Octopus Avenue. Ting-Ting leaned a little closer. Her eyes were fixed on the palm of my hand.

"Do you know what this is, Ting-Ting?" I asked, opening my hand so she could see clearly what it was.
"Uh...I think so. It's very pretty."
Ting-Ting stretched out her right hand tentatively towards my palm.
"I found it in Ro-Ro Gway-Gway's poop one day! Isn't it cool?"

Guilty Stomachs and Successful Invitations

Ting-Ting's hand stopped in midair.[8] This time her eyebrows had risen all the way up to her wavy bangs.[9]

"Kobi! You're kidding, right?"

"Nope. It's true. I swear. He must've swallowed it somehow. Auntie Guo says it's from New Zealand." [10]

"Ro eats New Zealand poop?!" asked Ting-Ting in her excitement.

Then she shook her head and burst out laughing at her own silly question. I laughed too.

When we eventually stopped, her hand stretched all the way over to mine. I could feel her artistic fingertips brush gently against my palm. She picked up the small wood carving that Ro had smuggled millions of miles in his internal luggage.

"New Zealand? Wow, what a find!"

"Yep. On the back you can see 'AVE THE WHA' and KAI RA' carved out at the bottom. Auntie Guo says 'Kaikora' is the name of a small town in New Zealand. It's famous for whale watching. She really is extremely knowledgeable, don't you think?"

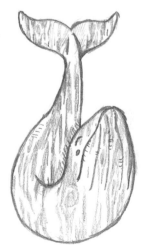

"...internal luggage..."

"So 'AVE THE WHAL' is...'Save the Whales?" asked Ting-Ting, turning over the carving and inspecting the small faded letters on the back.

"That's what Auntie Guo thinks. Do you like it?"
"It's beautiful."
"Then you can have it." I smiled.
"No, no Kobi, I couldn't..."
"No no's! I want you to have it. Actually, it was Ro's idea. He really loves the picture you drew of him. He wanted to say thank you, so we decided you'd like this the most. We figured you could wear it on a string necklace."

Ting-Ting's dark eyes lit up as she contemplated the prospect of owning such an exotic fashion accessory.
"Besides, a necklace would look much better on you than it would on us," I added. "It wouldn't suit us; our necks are too thick."
Ting-Ting's head rolled back as she shook with laughter again. Various customers in the shop turned around this time, staring at us for a short while. Then they continued their search for the perfect peach or nectarine.[11]

Ting-Ting looked around a little embarrassed, leaned even

Guilty Stomachs and Successful Invitations

closer and whispered, "Who told you your necks are too thick?"

"The bathroom mirror!" I chuckled.

Ting-Ting smiled and held the carving up to the light. She greedily inspected it from every angle. "Thanks Kobi. I love it. It's fabulous. And I think you need a new mirror," she smiled sweetly.

"Cool. Ro knew you would like it!"

"Please tell him I do. I love it! And I owe him a kiss!"

Ting-Ting looked around the shop, as if selecting something with a trained eye. "Well, since Christmas has come early this year," she said, "I won't let you leave without trying these in return..."

I could feel tiny beads of sweat forming on my thick neck as Ting-Ting walked to the front of the shop and selected half a dozen of the biggest, ripest, juiciest dragon fruits[12] she could find. I tried to protest but she wouldn't hear it. She fit them neatly into a bag and handed it to me with a broad, brilliant smile. Then she mentioned something about the purple ones being sweeter than the white ones, but I was thinking too much about dragons and destiny to notice. My heart was beating like crazy in my chest...I took a deep breath...took the plunge...

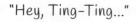

"Hey, Ting-Ting..."

"Uh-huh?"

"Do you want to meet some interesting dragons—I mean people—tomorrow afternoon?"

"Uh...okay, sure. Who are they?" she asked, still caressing the Maori[13] artifact between her delicate fingers.

"Just some foreign friends that we met yesterday at Milkshake's drink shop. They're from Switzerland."

"Wow, what an international day!" laughed Ting-Ting. "First New Zealand, now Switzerland. What other tricks do you have up your sleeve, Kobi?"

"That's the last one, unfortunately," I smiled.

I was a bit disappointed that I'd run out of surprises to give the girl I was in love with, but I was overjoyed that she accepted the invite. It was a dream come true. That I managed not to celebrate wildly right there in the fruit shop (like a desperate sailor who just sighted land after six months at sea) was one of the greatest accomplishments of my life.

"Great," I said, no longer worried about being cool or saying cool things. "In that case, you can come to our cabin tomorrow at five. Mr. & Miss Kloss are dying to meet Ro. Oh, and I really need your advice about something too."

Guilty Stomachs and Successful Invitations

註 解

1　片語：別太早就覺得很得意，或是事情完成前還是不要完全指望
　　能得到的後果較好；正確的諺語為：*'don't count your chickens
　　before they hatch'*

2　生物動因退化 , 生物降解 (詞彙 biodegrade=bio+degrade; 參
　　考 biology, grade, upgrade)

3　電動遊戲 literally 'electronic movement game'

4　榴蓮 literally 'pomegranate lotus'

5　私藏

6　暈船 (詞彙 seasick=sea+sick)

7　《少年 Pi 的奇幻漂流》裡面的那隻老虎 *Life of Pi* (2012)

8　半空中 (詞彙 middle, midnight, midday, midterm exam)

9　瀏海 also 'fringe' (Br.)

10　紐西蘭 literally 'button west orchid'

11　油桃 literally 'oil peach'

12　火龍果 literally 'fire dragon fruit'

13　毛利人 literally 'gross profit people'

Change

變

Chapter 22 / Sunday Afternoon

Bubbles

Once, when I was a little boy, Nai-Nai showed me how to blow a soap bubble for the very first time. I loved the first bubble I blew so much that I cried when it burst. Nai-Nai said I was being silly to cry over a bubble, because it hadn't actually burst. She said it had just changed into something else. When I asked her what it had changed into, Nai-Nai said that bubbles became the stuff that makes you sneeze. She said that nothing ever disappears. It just changes into something else. Whenever I sneeze, I think of bubbles and who first blew them. And what they became...

Tired

累

Chapter **23** / 🌧️ Later that Sunday Afternoon

Sorry

Sorry

On the way home from the fruit shop, I decided to drop by Mr. Wu's house to see if he'd heard about the scooter parked in the harbor. When I arrived, the farmer was outside in the vegetable garden singing a catchy love solo to himself and picking some ripe tomatoes. It was quite obvious that the chubby little shadow boxer was in pure ecstasy. The news that Officer Wang's scooter had been ridden into the sea pleased him so much, that he spent the entire morning singing to himself in the garden and drinking cheap champagne. He even bought a cigar, which he tried to smoke in celebration. Unfortunately, he had to give up the romantic notion of this purchase after a few minutes of coughing and spitting.

I tapped on the wire fence surrounding his yard to let him know that I was there.
Hearing the familiar iron jingle, Mr. Wu looked up cheerfully. I never thought I'd hear a chuckle coming out of Mr. Wu's mouth. It was as if he was about to leave for his honeymoon or some unforgettable expedition or something.
"Kobi, my boy! Come in! Come in!" he said. "Actually, I was just picking some juicy tomatoes for you and your grandfather! Aren't they beautiful? Add a pinch of salt and your tongue will do a rain dance."

He held up a large, red, round tomato and smiled proudly and generously all at once.

Needless to say, I wasn't really expecting this kind of friendly reception from a person who couldn't smile properly, so I stood in the gate for a while not knowing if I should believe my ears. "Come in, come in, child! Don't just stand there like a marble statue," he teased. "Anyway, I need you to help me finish filling these two baskets. One is for you and your grandfather. The other one has to be delivered to Brother Liao."

Now, of course I felt guilty about being rewarded for my role in the scooter conspiracy. But, that didn't stop me from helping Mr. Wu to finish putting together the two largest baskets of fresh produce I'd ever seen. Besides, as if by some miracle, the sight of cucumbers and spinach made me feel more and more innocent, and by the time we were done, I'd completely convinced myself that I actually deserved a reward. I don't think I was quite as happy as Mr. Wu was, but I whistled a happy tune all the way home nonetheless.

My excellent mood changed abruptly upon my arrival. Ye-Ye was coughing quite loudly again. His old eyes were watering and he was hunched over the back of his favorite armchair.

Sorry

I quickly ran over to him and tapped him several times on the back. This seemed to help and the coughing stopped. I helped him around the back of the chair and held him firmly by the shoulders as he sank into his familiar seat. Then I darted to the kitchen and returned with a glass of water and a napkin. I placed them on the small table next to the armchair and turned on the fan. Then I helped Ye-Ye sit up straight and stuffed one or two of the sofa cushions behind his back to prop him up. I retrieved the glass and the napkin and held both up to his mouth. When he had quenched his thirst, cleared his throat and wiped his mouth and eyes, Ye-Ye turned to me with a weak smile.

"You're a good lad, Kobi," he said, grateful for my assistance. "The best grandson any old man could ever hope for."

"You're not old, Ye-Ye" I said, trying to sound cheerful. "You're just tired."

"You're right, my boy. I'm not old. None of us get old. But our bodies do. Mine's much older than me."

"No it's..."

"Kobi. "I'm sorry about your parents, Kobi. I really am. Because of everything, you're actually older than your body. That's not how it should be. I'm so sorry."

I suddenly remembered the night before and how I had lied to Ye-Ye that morning over breakfast.

"Ye-Ye, I'm the one who has to say sorry. I wasn't being completely honest this morning. Forgive me!"

Ye-Ye raised an eyebrow and nodded as if to encourage me to continue.

"Ye-Ye, I...I did something last night that I'm not very proud of. I...I kind of Luckily, something that wasn't mine."

There was a pause as Ye-Ye blinked several times. He smoothed out one or two folds in his shirt with his frail, bony hands.

"That's okay, Kobi," he finally smiled, shifting his gaze and pointing to the coffee table. On it was lying the floppy gardening hat that I'd borrowed the evening before.

I couldn't believe my eyes. How the hat had ended up there, I had absolutely no idea. "But...how, Ye-Ye? When did..."

"That's not important Kobi. Belongings are not important. What's more important is that you willingly made a confession. That you chose to be honest. In this life, denial is so abundant. It's epidemic. All of us deny when we are at fault. It's too difficult for us to criticize ourselves. That's why admitting that you did something you're not proud of, is much harder than actually doing it or denying it. Harder than a raw chestnut, Kobi."

"But, I didn't mean the hat, Ye-Ye. I kind of moved something else too."

"That's alright, my boy. Whatever you did, confession is the first step to correcting your mistakes. And, when you correct your mistakes," said Ye-Ye winking at me and refolding his hands on his lap, "...that's when you grow."

Ye-Ye seemed to be a bit out of breath so I tried to motion to him to slow down. He paused for a short while before continuing.

"That's why I'm not worried about leaving you on your own Kobi, because I know you're growing all the time. I know you'll stay out of trouble or at least try to learn from it if you can't. I know you can handle the responsibility. You have tremendous potential, my boy...you can be anything you want...do anything you want...achieve anything you want... love anyone you want."

"Leaving me?" I asked as Ro came into the room with slow, deliberate movements like he knew what was about to happen.

"I'm just going to nap for a little while, Kobi my boy. I'm a little tired. And a little dizzy. When you get to my age— I mean when your body gets to this age—your battery sometimes just runs a little flat," he joked.

"Ye-Ye, you're not coming down with something, are you? You look a little pale. I can run out and pick up something at the drugstore if you like? Anything. Seriously, I'll be back in no time!"

Ye-Ye could tell how concerned I was and assured me again that it was just his 'battery.'

With a smile he added, "I just need to get some rest, Kobi, that's all. All of a sudden, I feel very, very sleepy. Would the best grandson an old man could wish for...mind bringing me a pillow?"

Boat

船

Chapter **24** / Monday

The Sea Welcomes an Old Friend

Ye-Ye never woke up from his nap. Early the next day when I got up for school, he was still lying under a woolen blanket in his favorite armchair. I stood there watching him for a long time. I couldn't move. It was like my legs were on strike. Finally, something told me that I had better call Dr. Qing and he came over at once.

"I'm so sorry, Kobi," he said, shaking his head solemnly, "there's no pulse."

I heard the words and saw the dentist's fingers on my grandfather's wrist, but it was as if the sounds and the images weren't really going all the way into my mind. Pulse. It's such a fragile word. As fragile as a dewdrop.[1] One day it just stops. Like a watch. It didn't feel like I was crying either, but I was. I'm not sure if turtles can cry, but I knew Ro was too. I didn't have to look.

"Don't worry, Kobi," said Dr. Qing putting his hand on my shoulder, "I'll take care of everything."

"Th...Thanks, Doc. Thanks. I'll just sit with him here for a while. He looks so peaceful."

A while turned out to be most of the day. Ro stayed close by the whole time. I felt too numb to go to school. My mind was a complete blank. When he heard what had happened, Milkshake came over immediately and kept me company too.

The Sea Welcomes an Old Friend

We didn't say anything though. We didn't do anything either. I never told him this, but it was nice to have another friend there with me. The silence was too hard to bear alone.

I didn't want to move from where I was seated, in case Ye-Ye woke up. To be honest, I knew he wouldn't. I knew Ye-Ye was gone. Or rather his body was gone. I tried to remember that he had lived a good life and would be happy wherever he was going next, but I still felt very empty inside. I guess worrying about good people who die is a complete waste of time, but maybe, deep down, we're just worrying about ourselves and whether we'll be okay without them.

My grandfather's final wish was to be buried at sea. I know this might seem strange to most people, but Ye-Ye thought most people were strange too. For him, fish had been feeding him his whole life and, like he said, it was time for him to feed them for a change. Besides, he had to find Nai-Nai anyway and show her the right way to heaven, otherwise she'd remain lost forever in her little boat.

His last wishes made perfect sense to me and the people who knew Ye-Ye. He didn't like big, complicated procedures that took up people's time. He valued it too much to deprive anyone else of it. He was a simple man and he liked things to be simple. Even dying.

That afternoon we wrapped his remains in plain white linen sheets and laid them down in his favorite rowboat. People from all around town came over to the cabin. They burned incense and said prayers. Milkshake told Mr. Kloss and his daughter Hannah what happened, and they also came to pay their respects. Ting-Ting and Hannah had a fierce crying competition as some of Ye-Ye's closer friends filled the boat with bunches of flowers and handfuls of seashells. I added some sweet potato leaves and a photo of Ye-Ye, Ro and I standing on the beach behind a medieval style sand castle. He would need something to look at on the way to the next place.

A certified nurse told us that she found a copy of Ye-Ye's birth certificate at the hospital and calculated his age. He was ninety-nine years old. He would have been one hundred in October. She said I took after him. The sun was starting to set. I had no tears left to cry.

Once we all said our goodbyes, we tied a rope to the front of the rowboat. Ro took the rope in his mouth and pulled

The Sea Welcomes an Old Friend

from the front, while I pushed from the back. We swam out with the boat into the sea. The water was perfectly calm, as if it was welcoming an old friend. Tiny waves tapped at the side of the vessel to say hello and gently rocked the floating coffin. The current guided us farther and farther out to sea. Approximately a hundred meters from the shore, I stopped and let go of the boat. I watched Ro continue pulling further and further away. The boat got smaller and smaller as I kept treading water.[2]

"Goodnight Ye-Ye. Give Nai-Nai a hug from me when you see her. Oh, and I promise...I'll never eat fish again."

I turned and swam back towards the rocky beach. When I gazed back once or twice, Ro was still heading for Turtle Island. For a brief moment, he looked happy about the fish, but he was too heartbroken for the feeling to last. The ceremony was over. I never saw Ye-Ye again.

註 解

1   露珠 literally 'dew pearl' (詞彙 dewdrop=dew+drop)
2   踩水 (游泳動作) 'to tread water'

Night

夜

Chapter **25** / ✩✩ Monday Night

Hands

Once everyone had left, I sat on my own on the beach for what felt like ages. Barefoot and calm, I was staring out towards Turtle Island. When the people we love are absent, clocks slow down. They mean nothing. We become patient. Maybe we're waiting for those people to come back. We don't care how long it takes.

Apart from the full moon reflecting on that endless surface, the sea was already as black as charcoal. However, I could still make out the faint outline of the island lying perfectly still on the horizon. It was unmovable, peaceful, eternal.

Ting-Ting, Dr. Qing and Milkshake were sitting some distance behind me on the sand in complete silence too; just waiting. Waiting for me to let go.

Night had arrived. Finally I noticed some far-off ripples in the water. A small head appeared out of the blackness and I tracked it drawing nearer and nearer. This was followed by the emergence of Ro's seven-ribbed shell in the white foam spilling onto the beach. I stood up to meet him, fetched the Ro-Mobile and walked over to where the water was crashing onto the sand.

Funerals are exhausting, especially for turtles. But I didn't think my best friend looked exhausted; he just looked very sad. He was too sad to be tired. He climbed onto the sled and I took the leash in my right hand. Slowly, I started towing him up towards the empty cabin. Dr. Qing, Milkshake and Ting-Ting came over to us. I paused for a while as the dental and flavor oracles[1] gave Ro several pats on the back. They showered him with praise for being so clever and so brave. Ting-Ting didn't say anything. Instead, she just bent down and stroked his head very lightly a few times before wiping a solitary tear from her eye. Then she stood up and took hold of my free hand. Her skin was as smooth as porcelain.

"Don't be dismayed, Kobi. Don't ever, ever be dismayed," she whispered. "We'll take care of you."

As we walked hand in hand up to the cabin, I remembered all the people that I would never stop loving.

"Funerals are exhausting, especially for turtles."

註解

---

1 神諭 literally 'divine instruction'

Star

星

Chapter **26** / Tuesday. Tuesday Week.
The Tuesday after that.

Searching

Not many people realize this, but surfing teaches you a lot of patience. Sometimes you have to wait for waves. Waiting. Waiting takes practice; not everyone is good at it. Sometimes I just sit on my board and look down into the water. I know you can't tell from a distance, but seawater is actually quite clear. You can see the bottom on most sunny days. And if the water's really clean, you can see small white shells resting on the black sand below. They look like stars against the night sky.

I heard somewhere that people in Africa believe that the stars are their ancestors.

Ye-Ye would make a great star. When I'm sitting on my board, I look for him in the dark sand. At night, I look for him in the dark sky.

"I look for him in the dark sand."

Write

寫

Chapter **27** / Two more Tuesdays after that

Blossoming

It's been a month since Ye-Ye set off to look for Nai-Nai. I still haven't thrown away or given away anything that belonged to him yet. It's too early. It wouldn't feel right. A clear picture of every individual line on his face still lingers in my mind. I don't think I'll ever get used to him not being there. Not because I'm lonely, but because Ye-Ye simply can't be replaced.

Officially, I was now living on my own, but to be honest, there was always someone at the cabin with me. Milkshake slept over most nights—he was practically rooming with me—and Ting-Ting visited everyday. Mr. Kloss dropped by numerous times before he went back to Europe and said I could contact him if I ever needed anything. Hannah came over whenever she could. By now, she and Milkshake were nearly as inseparable[1] as Ting-Ting and myself. Okay, they once almost broke up because they disagreed on which tea was best complemented by lemon, but they soon made up when Milkshake graciously admitted he was wrong. I don't think he honestly believed he was wrong, but it didn't matter because Hannah graciously overlooked this. She really is very nice that way.

Blossoming

Auntie Guo & Dr. Qing also came round to our cabin very often. When they did, they always brought lots of snacks and drinks, not to mention excellent conversation. Often, Auntie Guo arrived with her portable CD player, so we could listen to her favorite pianists together. She, Ting-Ting and Hannah really enjoyed each other's company. Being a firm believer in a well-balanced education, Auntie Guo started instructing them on all kinds of things. She taught them, for example, how to knit, do magic and purify their hearts and minds through meditation. And how to talk intelligently about everything ranging from cinema and opera, to psychology and sociology. Oh, and to distinguish between Mendelssohn, Brahms and Chopin[2] of course.

She also taught them that good looks are a lousy excuse for vanity and that it's always better to be humble. Even if you are as beautiful as a Japanese cherry blossom in full bloom (as the three of them were), it is still better to be humble. Needless to say, the girls benefited tremendously from this instruction. Milkshake and I were a bit worried that they would mature so rapidly that they'd quickly tire of us, but thankfully that hasn't happened yet. Mr. Xu says zebrafish[3] reach sexual maturity after just ten to twelve weeks. Wow.

On occasion, Auntie Guo would also bring over a large pile of books from the library. It was great. All of us would sit together outside the front door reading and sharing excerpts from some of the best novels ever written. Dr. Qing loves *Dream of the Red Chamber*[4] the most. He's always reciting passages from it. Milkshake's addicted to detective novels involving lots of money, large ransoms and that sort of thing. Hannah—I think she's going to be a playwright one day—adores Shakespearean comedies and stories with mummies in them.

We also found out, much to our surprise, that Mr. Wu's favorite is science fiction. Why someone with an engineering background, a camel smile and a vegetable garden would go in for that sort of thing, puzzled all of us. But hey, each to his own, right? Once, when we did actually ask Mr. Wu about it, he said that space travel and monstrous aliens reminded him of his childhood. This statement naturally induced a stunned silence among his fellow book lovers, but none of us had the courage to ask what that meant exactly. His statement had only added to our curiosity, but he said one day he'd write his own book about it to explain. I'm no creative genius but I'm going to write my own book one day. Even if no one reads it. Like a diary. Everyone should write a book.

Blossoming

Speaking of Mr. Wu...he had by now appointed himself my main benefactor and made sure to pop in at least twice a week. This was in spite of his turtle allergy, so I appreciated it a lot. He always brought a fresh supply of fruit and vegetables from his garden. He said it was just a small reminder that life is far less enjoyable if you don't eat a balanced diet. I was very grateful for the reminder. Sometimes he teaches me how to grow all kinds of things— not just sweet potatoes—and sometimes we speak for hours about how I should never ever steal or displace anything again.

He also likes to talk about how I should forget all about boyhood now, and start to take control of domestic affairs. He says it's time to be 'the man of the house.' Now and then, especially when he's in a good mood, he still finds time to congratulate himself on parking a conscientious cop's patrol scooter in the ocean without even touching it. The whole episode still amuses him to this day. Even more than alien adventures.

As far as I know, Officer Wang has never viewed me as a suspect in the case of the vanishing scooter. Or, if he has,

he's never actually said anything to me about it. I see him
quite often nowadays. He comes around once in a while
to check up on me and see if I'm okay. During these visits,
he's never once confronted me or accused me of anything.
Milkshake says it's just because he doesn't have any proof
and that he's probably secretly watching me like a hawk. As
far as I can tell, Officer Wang is secretly watching everyone
like a hawk. I don't know why, but before I was scared of him
and now he makes me feel safe.

I still feel a bit bad about his scooter, of course. That's why I'm
teaching him how to surf for free. He really sucks at it, but
I've never seen someone have so much fun. I think it's the only
time he really can completely forget about crime and fines
and all that serious stuff. As soon as his feet touch the foam[5]
of the beginner board, he's like a little child all over again. I
wish his wife could see him that way. She never will though.
Like most Taiwanese women, she's a vampire when it comes
to sunshine. One day, when the time is right, I'll confess to
Mr. Wang and tell him exactly what happened that night in his
yard. When I do, Ye-Ye the star will be very proud.

Mr. Wang and his colleagues conducted several thorough
investigations into the scooter mystery. They explored all

the existing possibilities. Since there were lots of witnesses to verify that Brother Liao was nowhere near the Wangs' house that night, everyone suspected that the person who removed the patrol scooter from their yard was not the same person who parked it in the harbor. Everyone was convinced that there was a third party involved. Only five of us knew that it was me: myself, Mr. Wu, Milkshake, Ro and Ye-Ye's star.

In the end, since he couldn't prove who it was, the official statement Officer Wang issued to the local press didn't mention any third parties. Milkshake had a very reasonable theory about why this was the case, which I reckon showed a lot of social insight. He said that getting your scooter stolen and then drowned in the Pacific Ocean must constitute a terrible scandal for any respectable policeman. Especially if it was stolen by a teenager whose best friend is a turtle. A sleepwalking drunk with a long history of offences committing such a crime was almost just as humiliating, but at least there would be no turtles involved.

Milkshake also said that, maybe, Officer Wang was even worried that he'd get fired or have to resign if people knew what really happened. You see, Officer Wang always considered himself to be some kind of heroic modern-day sheriff. Maybe being the victim of this sort of robbery was just too humiliating. Milkshake's conclusion was therefore that, rather than make a big fuss about who and how many were really to be held accountable for the scandalous affair, Officer Wang preferred to just be silent about the whole thing. It's not that he became the least talkative cop in history or something, but nobody ever heard him say 'the Law shall prevail' again, that's for sure.

Whatever anyone was theorizing, it was obvious that the incident was still a sensitive issue for Officer Wang. That's why he had to depend on a variety of ways—laughing too loudly whenever anyone mentioned the incident or bottling up his anger—to convince others that it wasn't really a sensitive issue. The surfing helped for that too, I must say.

Anyway, fortunately, all was forgiven in the end when Brother Liao bought him a brand new scooter and an upgraded baseball mailbox with his lottery winnings.[6]

註解

1　分不開的, 不可分離的 (詞彙 inseparable=in (否定的)+separate+able; 參考 innumerable, invaluable)

2　孟德爾頌, 布拉姆斯, 蕭邦

3　斑馬魚 (詞彙 zebrafish=zebra+fish)

4　《紅樓夢》 literally 'red building dream'; a famous Chinese novel

5　泡沫橡膠 beginner surfboards consist largely of a composite foam to increase buoyancy

6　(在比賽或打賭中) 贏得的錢 (詞彙 win, innings)

New

新

Chapter **28** / The Tuesday after that

Hats

Oh, sorry, I forgot to mention the lottery, didn't I? Now, you probably won't believe this story, but I'm going to tell it anyway. You see, after the patrol scooter in the sea incident, Brother Liao was kind of a changed man. Somehow, he'd finally realized that, apart from compromising his own health, he was bound to be arrested or killed—or both—if he continued with his favorite addiction. As a result, he vowed never to drink a single drop of alcohol again. From that day on, he would, like most of his compatriots, be a proud TV addict only.

We all respected him a lot for making such a sound life choice. And fate, always happy to encourage those that can cure themselves, smiled on him for making this very sensible decision. Or, perhaps it was his aboriginal ancestors that were doing the smiling, I'm not quite sure. Either way, the smiling started the very first time Brother Liao went to the High Life on the corner, and purchased a bottle of water instead of beer or imported whisky. He kept the receipt in order to commemorate turning over a new leaf and vowed that from that moment onwards, he was going to be a decent member of society. Two weeks later, the new Brother Liao discovered that the souvenir had won him two million bucks in the National Receipt Lottery. Isn't life strange?

Naturally, this turn of fortune sparked years of controversial debate in the village. Far more than abortion, racism, ethnic cleansing, homosexual marriage, heterosexual divorce, divine conception or political corruption ever did. It was a hot topic. Local inhabitants debated for hours about whether a man of Brother Liao's once loose morals deserved such a blessing. It was like he was being rewarded for his sins. None of this debating or controversy seemed to bother Brother Liao though. He was a millionaire! Suddenly a new man, he wandered around the town as if he'd been free of budgets and moral judgment since the end of the last dynasty. He acted as if he could afford anything under the sun. He even took up civilized hobbies like jogging and stamp collecting to complete the revolution. I think success makes you want to collect things and exercise more, but I'm not sure.

He also made use of the miracle money to buy an LCD[1] TV for himself and his mother, as well as the new scooter and mailbox for Officer Wang. The latter's pride wanted to turn down the offer, but his wife wouldn't let him. Then Brother Liao, following some extensive and equally revolutionary restorations to his old store, created the best new surf shop on the whole east coast. Outside the store, he had a huge new cage made for Mr. Beak. Inside, he placed a couple of leather sofas and some luxurious imported cushions for Mr. Claw to claw to pieces. The walls were expertly painted by Ting-Ting. She also helped to decorate the place with tribal artifacts as a tribute to Brother Liao's aboriginal heritage. Brother Liao proudly named the shop 'New Waters'. The logo was a turtle riding the perfect wave into a golden sunset. Then he had 'New Waters' and the logo tattooed on his left calf. Milkshake didn't get a tattoo, but he did invest in the store, so I guess that makes him an associate.

Not long after the best new surf shop on the east coast had opened, Brother Liao offered me a part-time job at New Waters giving surf lessons. It was a very attractive proposal. I didn't hesitate to accept it. Brother Liao seemed pleased that I did. My first day on the job, he told me in his own unique way how happy he was that I was working for him.

"You're lucky to be here, Kobi," he said.

"Yes, Boss."

"Basically it's just because no one else applied for the position. You know that, don't you?"

"Yes, Boss. Shortage of applicants."

"Like Ro-Ro Gway-Gway for instance," he complained, "he's actually far more qualified for the position, but sadly he

didn't submit an application."

"No, he didn't, Boss."

"You're a lucky guy, Kobi."

"I know, Boss."

"So am I, Kobi. Call me 'Boss' again and you're fired."

I think I was also sort of Brother Liao's apprentice, because he taught me how to paint surfboards, repair cracks and chips in them and make accurate measurements for shaping new boards. Giving lessons was easy. All I had to do was show beginners how to paddle like they were being chased by a shark, and how to stand with their bums to the side like a baseball batter. After that, I just had to share one or two of the other requirements for surfing (like a bit of bravery, years of practice and a healthy dose of respect for the ocean) and my job was done. It was also nice to have some extra pocket money and not be broke all the time. I could finally start saving up for college.

It was nice to get Milkshake the economist off my back as well. I was getting a bit tired of him preaching to me about the benefits of cash flow,[2] and the dangers of poverty and unemployment. Brother Liao bought me some new surfing gear, too. I was over the moon[3] about that! He bought the gear on condition that I didn't share any of it, or see it as a debt that I had to pay off. On top of that, I was outfitted with official surf shop attendant merchandise. New Waters shorts, t-shirts and a black waterproof jacket. I even have a New Waters cap with 'KOBI' and 'INSTRUCTOR' sewn in bright gold letters on the sides. The logo's in the front. For someone who never wears hats, I really do love that cap.

Speaking of hats... To this day, I have no idea who was responsible for the only piece of concrete evidence in the scooter drowning mystery, being returned safely to the owner. Mr. Wu never mentioned it. Milkshake didn't seem to know anything about it either. Besides, he was probably too busy that night thinking about his first meeting with Hannah to have followed me down Octopus Avenue looking for any clues I'd left behind. Oscar? (I had after all suggested a girlfriend for him, so he owed me a favor.) Little Shu? (Like I said before, she knows everything and is always everywhere.) Ro?! (He'd want to protect his best friend wouldn't he?) Nai-Nai?? (Had she found her way back and helped out her only grandson?) Officer Wang himself? (Had Ye-Ye made him promise not to do anything about it until I had willingly confessed?) Who knows? Not even my Sherlock mind could figure this one out.

Anyway, the fact remains that someone—or something—had retrieved the hat and returned it to my grandfather. It really was a riddle. Life is strange. Mysterious. There are so many unknowns that can never be adequately accounted for. Like a huge puzzle with lots of missing pieces. A puzzle that you have to piece together in the dark. That's why trying to analyze it too much can only lead to headaches and confusion. Sometimes, it's best just to be grateful for the pieces you have.

One thing I was very grateful for was that I was constantly surrounded by all these great friends who loved me and wanted to protect me. Since Ye-Ye had left, I seemed to appreciate them even more. I cherished all the time that we could spend with each other. Some nights, we'd all get together and have a big vegetarian barbecue on the beach. We'd roast tomato and pickled onion sandwiches, along with some homemade stinky tofu. For an extra treat, we'd wrap sweet potatoes and giant Japanese mushrooms up in some lettuce leaves. Yummy!

The vegetarian barbecue was my idea. Since promising Ye-Ye that I'd never eat fish again, I decided to extend that to all animals. That way, there was no chance that I'd indirectly be eating Ye-Ye or someone else. Secondly, my best friend was an animal, so it kind of made sense. Everyone else was unanimous in saying that my being vegetarian in memory of Ye-Ye was an excellent idea. In fact, I've never seen them eat meat since either. We made an exception for Ro because he can't plant vegetable gardens and barbecue mushrooms. Besides, someone has to eat all the jellyfish, otherwise they'd take over the planet.

"I'm tired of eating dead animals anyway," said Mr. Wu one night when we started on our frozen banana dessert. "I'm sure aliens don't. Besides, sausages used to give me a constant headache for some reason. And, I chipped my tooth once on a lamb chop. From now on, I'll get my protein from nuts and beans. Yes, starting tomorrow, I'm going to campaign for the rights of animals. Especially the ones we used to eat!"
Mr. Wu paused as we all cheered this noble sentiment.
"I'm only human," he added modestly, "so I will miss tuna a little. And fish eggs. And maybe some crispy pork fat or a nice greasy slice of bacon. Luckily I'm as stubborn as a mule, otherwise someone might tempt me with one of those!"
Ting-Ting nearly split her sides laughing when she heard

the vegetable farmer express this conviction. She only realized that it wasn't a joke when she caught a glimpse of the very serious expression on Mr. Wu's face half a minute later.

"I...Uh...I was thinking of becoming a vegetarian chef, actually," she said quickly, choking back her chuckles.

This seemed to work because Mr. Wu finally smiled his awkward camel smile.

I don't miss eating dead animals either.

On clear nights, after dessert, Hannah plays her guitar and Auntie Guo tells us stories from all over the world. Sometimes the stories are about the stars and galaxies. I can sense that it disappoints Mr. Wu somewhat that there's always lots of Greek[4] and Roman[5] mythology in the stories and not one single spaceship, but he nevertheless still looks happy listening to Auntie Guo tell her long and complex tales. Dr. Qing, on the other hand, looks more than happy to listen to Auntie Guo for any reason whatsoever. My suspicions that the two of them were secretly in love weren't confirmed until many months later. That's when the doctor finally made a reservation at a very expensive restaurant and proposed. Two days later, the librarian, having successfully persuaded him to shave off his little beard and do all the cooking at home, finally said yes.

When I'm not looking at the storyteller, I look up at the stars. I always think of Ye-Ye when I do. He and Nai-Nai must be at least half-way to heaven by now, surely. I hope they can look down and see us all together remembering them. I also want Ye-Ye to see that I'm not lonely and that I have many friends and caretakers to help me and support me now that he's no longer here. I want him to know that I'm safe and that I'll be totally fine. I also want him to know that I'm thankful for all the sacrifices he made for me. Above all, I hope he can see that Ro and I miss him every single day.

註 解

1 液晶顯示 (詞彙 liquid crystal display)
2 現金流轉 (詞彙 cash, flow)
3 片語：欣喜若狂 *'to be over the moon'*
4 希臘 literally 'hope wax'
5 羅馬 literally 'bird net horse'

Island

島

Chapter **29** Wednesday, Thursday, Friday

Outnumbered

News that a typhoon was just around the corner, swept across the town like wildfire[1] this morning. According to the previous night's weather forecast, it was heading right for us and was supposed to touch down on Saturday evening. It wasn't quite summer yet, and already the first typhoon of the season was on its way. I hope someone invents something to replace coal and oil soon, because the weather is getting stranger and stranger each year.

Now, if there's anyone reading this that has never experienced a typhoon, let me describe it for you. Basically, the arrival of a typhoon just means the arrival of really dreadful weather for two or three days. Raging winds and driving rain. Picture the most windy, rainy, flight-grounding, window-rattling two or three days you can possibly imagine. Then multiply it by a hundred.

Sure, if you're lucky, you get to stay at home and don't have to go to school. But, the other side of the coin is that you have to worry about your ceiling leaking, the first floor flooding and big fat tree branches crushing your car or scooter like a grape. If you're really unlucky, all three of these things happen and the typhoon decides that its arrival will be on a weekend. This time we were going to be really unlucky.

The only good thing about typhoons is that you can bet they'll send out some great waves one or two days before they get there themselves. It's almost like they're trying to apologize for all the destruction and inconvenience they're about to cause. During the typhoon, by the way, the waves are not at all wonderful. Don't even think about trying to catch them. During that time, it's like the sea is angry about all the inconvenience as well and just wants to destroy anything in its path. It could easily destroy you and me too, so if I were you, I'd stay well clear of the water when any typhoon comes knocking. Otherwise, it might lead to some disastrous consequences. If, for some reason, you want to prove how fearless you are, try and steal some green peppers from Mr. Wu's garden instead. He's scary, but he's not quite as destructive.

Yesterday we had some of the nicest waves I've ever surfed. Sure, the horizontal line-up—the line of surfers waiting alongside one another for the first batch of waves to break—was pretty crowded at the main beach. I lost count at 58 boards. But, everyone was having so much fun that all the 'traffic' didn't matter. Dr. Qing had lent Ting-Ting his digital camera for the day, so she and Hannah had a very pleasant time sitting on the pier nearby gossiping and taking

photographs and videos of all the wave riders. Milkshake,
who preferred badminton and needed a good excuse not
to surf such enormous waves, volunteered to be their
bodyguard. In addition, he brought along two sophomore
finance books, a biography on Terry Guo[2] and a calculator.
Just in case he got bored with protecting them from danger,
you know. Indulging in some projections concerning future
inflation figures or the returns on his many investments was
always a sure cure for Milkshake's boredom.

As usual, Ro was the star of the show and he hadn't
even entered the water yet. One or two journalists from
Taipei had even come down to see the surfing turtle for
themselves. Oh, and to interview his orphaned owner.
Leatherbacks are an endangered species (only a few
thousand adults remain in the wild), so it was even rumored
that a renowned TV producer was also on the way to check
us out. However, I can't say I was delighted to hear that.
The last thing in the world I want to be is a celebrity, so this
was all a bit embarrassing.

To be honest, I wasn't keen on Ro and I being exposed to
too much media attention either. Maybe I was just worried
that someone would come along and take him away from me.

Besides, I also had the notion that bad things tend to happen to famous people. I mean, look at Ah Bian[3] or Michael Jackson[4] for example. As far as I could tell, publicity could only bog you down. Fame and fortune are more dangerous than a moody hippo, if you ask me. Milkshake suggested that Ro could get rich starring in some advertisements, but the thought of my best friend advertising washing powder or shampoo nearly gave me a fever. Before long, multiple advertisers and agents would be involved and life, my clothes and my hair would never be the same again.

But, I'm afraid Ting-Ting was probably right. There was no way we could avoid curious interviewers and press agencies forever. I mean, a pet leatherback that loves surfing...that's every journalist's dream, right? Soon they'd be broadcasting Ro's story on newscasts all over the country. It was a scary thought.

"You might as well use all the media coverage to make people more aware about the plight of the leatherback turtle, Kobi", Ting-Ting had said this morning. "And about water pollution and such things."

"She's right, Kobi," echoed Hannah. "You should instruct those reporters to make sure and tell everybody that turtles should be eating jellyfish instead of manmade[5] junk!"

This afternoon's waves were even better. More and more people had flocked to the beach. There were lots of beginners in the water too, and myself and the other locals had to make sure to keep a safe distance from them. I think it's terrific that they want to learn how to surf, but an out-of-control surfboard can be quite dangerous—especially if it's someone else's! Brother Liao always used to say, in-between drags of a cheap cigarette, that surfer newbies[6] are accidents waiting to happen. But, after a few scooter incidents of his own, he didn't mention the 'a' word so much anymore.

My muscles were still a bit stiff from all the surfing yesterday, but I knew Ro would never forgive me if we missed out on these perfect conditions. After thoroughly waxing the Banana and securely fastening the leash to my ankle, I found myself paddling out again behind him. I wasn't surprised to see one or two foreigners with short boards in the water as well. They usually surface when there are bigger waves. However, I couldn't believe my eyes when I saw Auntie Guo sitting on a bright pink long board right in the middle of the lineup.

"Auntie Guo!" I shouted excitedly as I began to paddle over to her. "You surf?!"

The only answer she supplied was a big beaming smile

before turning back to see if any catchable waves were approaching. Just before I reached her side, one of these did arrive and before I knew it, Auntie Guo and her bright pink long board were speeding away from me towards the beach, elegantly weaving through all the newbies with a gentle sway of her hips.

My immediate reaction was to secretly pinch myself. I had to make sure that I wasn't dreaming or imagining this remarkable transformation from librarian into watersports[7] fanatic. Then I bent over double on my board with laughter. When I could finally sit up, I broke into spontaneous applause. "Woo-hoo! Auntie Guo! You're awesome!"

Still riding the same wave, she answered with a smile and raised her arms far above her head in triumph. Then she started waving to everyone she passed in the water. Not like a politician who waves to strangers during an election campaign. More like someone who can't hide her happiness and has to let it out. Wants to share it. Like a kid with a massive ice cream cone in their hand. Or a dog whose owner is coming home. Surfers call this feeling being 'stoked'.[8] They say it reverses the aging process and brings out the kid in you. I think this is true because, as loud cries and cheers rose up from all over the line-up, Auntie Guo looked younger and more athletic than ever. I think Ro was a little envious of all the attention she had suddenly attracted. He also didn't want to be unexpectedly outdone[9] by a librarian, so he quickly followed suit[10] on a wave of his own. After all, as the best surfer on the island, he had a reputation to live up to.

The pain in my muscles had completely disappeared and it was time to start catching some waves of my own. I'm not sure if it was the good conditions or the fact that the two most important ladies in my life (Ting-Ting and Auntie Guo of course) were there to watch me, but today was easily the best I'd ever surfed. I still couldn't keep up with Ro of course, but it was the first time I felt I could actually anticipate the size, shape and direction of every wave. Before, I used to just sit passively[11] and hope that the odd wave would come my way. Today, I was actively scouting the horizon for any potential rides and positioning myself accordingly. I'd never caught so many good waves in one session. It was a great feeling. I was glad that Ro could see it too.

I had so much fun that I stayed in the water all afternoon and even beyond the cloudy sunset. Slowly but surely, the waves and lifeguard whistles died down. The large crowd of surfers and spectators started to disappear one by one. Shadows began to lengthen and dusk was gradually smothering us in its silent embrace. Eventually, I saw Auntie Guo catch her last wave of the day as well, and I waved back as she held up her hand on the shore. Since it was too dark to take any more photos, Ting-Ting and Hannah had also packed up their things and called to me from the pier to join them at the surf shop. I held up one hand and spread out my fingers to indicate that I'd be out in five minutes.

By now, the sea was perfectly calm. There was no sign of a typhoon coming at all. The calm before the storm. The first stars were coming out and only a handful of surfers were left scattered at a distance from one another along the empty lineup. The town lights started flickering in the distance. I could see the surfer closest to me, a foreigner who was about twenty yards away, start paddling back towards the beach. He smiled and motioned to me to join him. Then, in an Australian accent, he said that I shouldn't be too greedy. He was right—it was time to call it a day.

In the fading light I could just make out a single approaching wave and I promised myself that this would be the last ride. Just as I was about to set off, I spotted Ro's smooth spoon-

shaped head pop up above the dark water. At least, I thought
it was Ro. Seconds later I saw an identical head emerge
just a few feet away. Then a third. I think it was a female. I
wasn't sure though, I almost couldn't tell them apart. Three
Ro's? Three turtles! I'd never been outnumbered by turtles
before...

Suddenly I felt something brush the sole of my right foot
and I realized that Ro had been by my side all along. Looking
down, I could see his familiar eyes staring up at me, even
darker than the night sea. I saw a single star reflected in
each but they looked sorrowful again. Like when Ye-Ye had
left us.
"They've come to get you, haven't they, Ro?" I said softly.
Salty water gently tapped the side of my board and my best
friend's jaw. I tried to swallow back the tears but they were
already flowing down my cheeks. "Where are they taking
you? Is it far away?"
Ro-Ro Gway-Gway placed his front flippers on the side of
the Banana and pulled himself up a little out of the water.
His three companions and escorts swam closer, circled once
around us and then started heading off in the direction of
Turtle Island. Ro opened his mouth slightly as if his aim was
to answer all my questions at once. He tapped twice on my

board with his cheek and smiled his perfect turtle smile. Then, he slowly vanished beneath the surface. As I looked back one last time, four heads were swimming out to Turtle Island.

I know he'll be back, but for now, the others need him.

註 解

1 像野火迅速 *'to spread like wildfire'* (詞彙 wildfire=wild+fire)
2 郭台銘 Foxconn founder and one of the richest people in Taiwan
3 阿扁 nickname for disgraced former Taiwanese president (陳水扁)
4 麥可 · 傑克森
5 人工的 (詞彙 manmade=man+made)
6 菜鳥 literally 'vegetable bird'; novice, rookie or beginner
7 詞彙 watersports=water+sports
8 熱情洋溢 , 非常開心
9 不甘示弱 *'not want to be outdone by someone'* (詞彙 outdo=out+do)
10 片語：跟著做 , 照別人的方式去做 , 學樣 'to follow suit', to act in turn or act accordingly. (詞彙：原來的用法是從撲克牌 (尤其橋牌) 開始的 , 意思是按照對方發的紙牌組而發牌。一副紙牌 (a pack / deck of cards) 裡面有四個 'suits'：spades (黑桃) , hearts (紅心) , diamonds (方塊) 和 clubs (梅花) 。
11 被動 passively (詞彙 passive)

Write

寫

Chapter **30** / ☀ A Saturday Too

The End. Maybe

On clear days, Ting-Ting and I like to sit on the beach as the sun goes down. (By the way, she's more beautiful than ever.) She usually has a sketchpad in her lap and a paintbrush in her left hand. Yep, she's creating her next masterpiece, a picture of Ro and I, the two people she admires most in the world, making friends with the waves...

We're sitting facing Turtle Island. That's where I want to be when my best friend comes back to me. He looks a lot like an island himself, actually. If you see him, let me know...